A Mother Lode of Murder
A Virginia City Mystery

Janice Oberding

Copyright © 2020 Janice and Bill Oberding

All rights reserved.

ISBN: 9781082052668

One

No one ever wakes up thinking *this will be my last day on earth*. Mary Hanlon didn't. She slept like the dead she was soon to join right up to the time Rose woke her up with bad news.

"What do you want?" Mary asked.
"Maude says for you to go." Rose said.
Mary misunderstood and leapt out of bed, yelling. "The sun's still shining. Why do we have customers this time of day?"
"You're to leave at once."
"What sort of prank--"
"Maude says get out!"
"You're lying."
"You're causing too much trouble. You're not bringing in enough money to warrant the food you eat every day." Rose hissed. Her eyes sparkling with cruelty she added, "Not to mention all the whiskey you drink up."
"I haven't been feeling so good of late." Mary sobbed.
"Not our concern."
"Maude and me, we're friends!" Mary said.
Rose stiffened, "You? Why would she want to be a friend with the likes of you? What can you do for her?"
"But what am I to do?" Mary demanded.
"If it's a handout you want you'll have to go see the Daughters of Charity."
"It's that smelly old sourpuss I refused last night

isn't it?" Mary asked.

Ignoring the question, Rose said, "Maude's been carrying you on your room and board long enough. What happens when the others find out she's letting you slide?" She gazed out the window then back at Mary. "The Silver Window is the best brothel in Virginia City. Our clients demand the best! We must make room for girls who can pay their way." She stared at Mary pointedly, "Those that still have their looks and can behave themselves, that's what Maude wants."

"But I have no place to go!"

Rose turned from her. They were all the same.

"You'll go someplace. Your kind always does. Now get your things together and be done with it. We don't want you causing a commotion and upsetting the others."

The others were Bridget, Nora, Kate and Louise. Mary didn't like any of the selfish doxies. She was certain none of them would mind her leaving. She'd known Maude a long time. And now she was being tossed out.

She reached for the chamber pitcher and poured water into the basin. Splashing her face, she said, "Leave me be and I'll get out of here that much sooner." If she was to cry, it would not be in front of this evil old woman.

"Don't take all day. Wing Li needs to clean the room." Rose said shutting the door behind her. Mary dressed and quickly tossed what little she owned into her ragged woolen purse. She pulled Maude's silver flask from the dresser drawer. She would take it with her. She might want a drop of whiskey and Maude had plenty of money to buy another.

Bundled up in her tattered woolen shawl Mary stomped out the front door and down the steps.

Tears stung her eyes as she stumbled out onto the road, absently holding her skirts from the winds that whipped at her. Maude had tossed her out like an old shoe and she vowed to never forgive her for it.

She would cross the canyon to Dayton. And as the day wore on she trudged deeper into the canyon. With darkness falling across Virginia City she stopped and leaned against a large boulder. Nothing mattered except pulling her shoes off. They were too small and narrow. Friction had worn away the heels and toes of her stockings. Large blisters rose on her heels. Her toes were red and raw. She rubbed her aching feet and regretted not buying that new pair of boots last spring.

She pulled the flask from her purse and drank freely. Maude owed her at least a drink. She settled against the boulder and pulled her shawl tighter around her bony shoulders.

An angry wind blew across the canyon. It would only get colder as the night wore on. She gulped the whiskey, letting its warmth flow through her. She would sleep here on the ground tonight and hopefully find a place in Dayton tomorrow. She settled against the jutting boulder and drifted off to sleep as the full moon rose higher in the sky.

Angry voices woke her. She sat upright and listened intently. She recognized those voices. As the conversation grew louder, fear surged through her. They would surely kill her if they knew she had heard their secret.

Mary arched her body against the boulder and stared up at a sky as black as the rich velvet coats wealthy gentlemen wore during the cold months. Issuing a silent prayer to the God who had long ago forgotten her, she noticed for the first time in years just how many stars sparkled across the night sky.

She drank the last drop of whiskey and listened. Only silence…they were gone…and she was safe. And then, the wracking cough rose up in her throat. A malady she had suffered most of her life, the hoarse barking cough could not be stopped once started. If only she had a drop or two of laudanum.

Desperate to stifle the cough, Mary tore at her scarf, stuffing a corner in her mouth.

The cloth was dry and bitter in her mouth. Her heart pounded against her chest as she coughed again…and again. Silence on the other side of the boulder, she was alone…and she was safe. But Mary Hanlon was wrong. Dead wrong. She remembered a prayer just as a pair of strong hands gripped her by the neck, silencing her cough forever.

Two

Chief Dolan settled into his old rocker with a steaming cup of coffee, a fresh cigar, and a copy of the Territorial Enterprise. All he wanted to do was spend his morning here reading the newspaper in the warmth of the potbelly stove.

He might have done so if not for the two men who stood panting before him.

"There she was all stiff and grey looking. I right near tripped over her." One of the men gasped.

"Dead as can be," the other man added.

Dolan listened without interrupting. There were days that he wanted to step down, give the job to someone else and be done with. This was one of them.

His presence was required, and there was no getting around it. He waited until the men had nothing more to add, then he held up his hand for silence.

"Whereabouts did you find her?"

"Like I said, she's by that big rock that points toward town. We was just heading out to--"

Dolan nodded impatiently. "I know the place. If that's all, you boys can be on your way."

After they'd gone, Dolan crushed his cigar, drained his cup and said, "Charlie my boy, you best run on over to the coroner and tell him we got business out in the canyon."

At the stable they saddled their horses and headed out toward Six-Mile Canyon with the coroner following in his wagon. Neither man spoke. When they reached the large boulder Charles dismounted and bent over the dead woman who lay sprawled in a thick patch of sagebrush. He brushed snow from her face, revealing ugly red marks that encircled her neck.

"Freeze to death did she?" Dolan asked hoping this death was anything but a murder.

"By the look of these marks around her neck she was strangled." Charles said, reaching to grab hold of something that was partially under the body.

"What's that?" Dolan asked.

"Looks like a flask." Charles said, holding it up for Dolan to examine.

"That belongs to Maude Banning," Dolan said. "See the tiny M and the B?"

The coroner stooped, examined the dead woman's neck and eyes, and said, "You're right, Bowling, she was strangled."

Dolan eased himself down from his horse for a closer look at the dead woman. "Well I'll be damned! That's Mary Hanlon from up at the Silver Window."

"She appears to have been dead a couple of days." The coroner said as he and Charles carefully loaded the body into his wagon. He stopped and looked at Dolan. "Okay if I take her?"

"All right by me. You done here Charlie?" Dolan asked.

"If it's all the same to you Chief, I'd like to take some time and look around here a bit longer. See what I can find" "
. Silently cursing old age and his rheumatism, Dolan painfully mounted his roan.

"Fine by me. See you back in town."

Charles watched the Chief's horse gallop out of sight then went back to sifting through the soil. With any luck there might be something more than the flask. Clouds fanned out from the sun and bright light flooded the area where he worked. He turned as a murder of crows squawked their way across the sky. Something was sparkling in the snow.

He bent and hurriedly dug at the snow, partially exposing a gold earring. He knew nothing about jewelry, but guessed this was not a cheap bauble. A fiery red ruby set in an intricate gold setting and encircled by tiny diamonds, the earring was exquisite. Rain clouds swept in obscuring the sun, another minute and he might never have seen the earring. He carefully placed it in his pocket and climbed on his horse.

Reining the horse, he headed toward town just as the rain started.

Three

Mrs. Noonan lit a fire in the stove and grumbled a good morning to her employers, Lottie Duckworth and Agnes Deeks, owners of the Duckworth and Deeks Rooming House. Fondly known as Ducks and Deeks to the many friends the two old ladies had here in Virginia City, the rooming house began as a way to assuage their lonely widowhoods. And that it had certainly done.

Lottie's nephew Charles had lived with her and her late husband since he was a baby. There was no question that he would live here at Ducks and Deeks, at least until he married. Rounding out the odd assortment of people who shared the large mansion with Lottie and Agnes was Benjamin, a retired Boston policeman who had chosen to live here when he discovered that Charles was an assistant to police chief Dolan. Next there was Sarah, a spinster who, as a young woman, had inherited the family fortune. Through frugality, she lived comfortably. Finally, there was Therese, a young school teacher.

None of them adhered to nineteenth century formalities in regards to their friendships. By virtue of living under the same roof, they had formed a tight familial bond.

While the others slept, Lottie and Agnes rose early every morning to oversee the breakfast preparations. This was not meant as any disrespect toward Mrs. Noonan's culinary abilities, but something the two old friends enjoyed.

They watched Mrs. Noonan deftly slice bacon

and place the thick strips in a large cast iron skillet. "Mind you, keep a sharp eye now. The biscuits should be out in a minute or two." She snapped at her assistant, a girl of about fifteen who yawned sleepily. Then glaring at her two employers she said, "We will be able to move about more freely once the ladies leave us."

A hint, the *ladies* might own the rooming house, but the kitchen was her domain. Lottie and Agnes, poured their coffee, and left the cook and her assistant to their work.

At the dining table, Agnes gathered her shawl tighter around her shoulders. "Where has the summer gone? Snow will be on the ground before we know it. It seems ages since we helped Charles with a case. "

Gazing out the rain covered window at the skeleton of her prized lilac bush, Lottie said. "It has been awhile."

"And that's a pity." Agnes said. "What we need is another murder to solve. Nothing else seems to pull us out of the doldrums.

Lottie nodded. "I agree. But all the same dear, it seems rather callous of us wishing for the death of another. "

Charles woke later than usual. With the wind hurling rain against the bedroom window, he thought of Chief Dolan, and of the many tasks waiting for him at the Virginia City Police Department. One of those would be solving the murder of the woman in the canyon without neglecting his other duties. His thoughts were quickly dispelled by the aroma of coffee and frying bacon wafting up from the kitchen. He was hungry. And breakfast would soon be ready. Deciding not to tell the others about the murder just yet, he kicked the covers off, pulled himself out of bed and hurriedly dressed.

Charles slid into his chair next to Therese and listened as his aunt the others discussed the recent death of their old friend Theodore Eldons and his funeral being held on this day.

Sarah filled her cup and said, "Poor Dan. He's been nursing his father-in-law for all these months while that wretched wife of his gallivants across Europe. Not many men would permit that behavior."

Agnes glared at her. "Why must you say such things? Miriam is a warm and wonderful human being. I pity Dan, of course I do. But Miriam is enjoying herself in Europe and not even knowing that her father has passed on."

"You're very quiet this morning, dear." Lottie said to Charles.

"The Chief has a lot of work for me today." He said.

"Not enough to keep you from Mr. Eldons' funeral I hope." She said.

He slid an egg into his plate and mashed its soft yellow yolk. "Don't worry Aunt Lottie. I'll be there for Dan."

"Speaking of Dan, he will probably deny it, but Miriam must have known how sick old Theodore was." Sarah sniffed. "But then poor Dan's a fool if you ask me."

No one had, but everyone at the table bit their tongues rather than point this fact out to her.

Four

Freezing rain came in torrents as mourners climbed into their carriages. Wind swept up from the canyon shaking signs and rattling shingles free. C. Street became a swamp as the funeral procession started its slow journey toward the cemetery. Black plumed horses pulled the mourners' carriages through the thick sludge.

They cautiously stepped from their carriages, the ladies trying to hold their long skirts above the mud. The coffin bearing Theodore Eldons' body was carefully taken from the hearse and carried to the awaiting grave. Mourners gathered beneath their umbrellas, holding on to them tightly against the wind's fierce pull.

Charles was here for only one reason. And that was to comfort his friend Dan Waters, Eldons' scarecrow skinny son-in-law.

"Sorry Dan," Charles said. "He was a fine man."

Waters' face was ashen, his brow lined with deep furrows. He shook, reminding Charles of clothes on a windy wash day. "Most kind Charles," he muttered. "I only wish that Miriam were here to help me."

I'll just bet you do, Charles thought. If the rumormongers were right, Miriam Waters selfishly spent her father's and her husband's money like it was sand. Life with her could not be easy for a man like Dan. When she grew bored with Virginia City and her responsibilities, she ran away to Europe leaving them to fend for themselves. This time she'd merrily skipped out without so much as a good-bye.

Even the self-centered Miriam would waste no time in returning home at the news of her father's death. In the meantime, the weak kneed Dan would have to wait. Charles consoled him with another pat on the shoulder. He had said all that he could to ease the man's pain.

Benjamin gave Dan a quick slap on the back saying, "Be strong, man."

The women came next, encircling Dan and offering kindness and help during his time of mourning. Charles watched with fascination as Dan's lips quivered and tears welled up in his eyes.

You poor bastard he thought, turning away from the other's display of unabashed weakness.

Five

News traveled fast. At least as fast as the undertaker's wife could get to the Comstock Book store and share what she'd heard about the dead woman out in the canyon. The town's men might gather at the saloons. But the women usually gathered at the book store. The love of reading and gossip brought them here. And today there was plenty of gossip to impart.

Out of breath the gossiper plopped down in the

rocking chair reserved for customers. "Did you hear? They found a dead woman out in the canyon. "

She didn't have to say another word. She had the full attention of Agnes and Lottie.

"Murder?" They asked, forgetting their new books for a moment.

Thus encouraged, the gossiper told everything she knew which was very little. But it was enough to spark their interests.

The notion that he was coming home for a respite from the day's crimes, was quickly dispelled as he came through the door.

"At the book store today there was talk about a dead woman out in Six-Mile Canyon. " Lottie greeted him.

With the others following on his heels he sat down at the dinner table.

"The undertaker's wife," Charles sighed.

"Is it true?" Agnes asked.

"Yes, but there's not much to go on." He said scooping roast beef and potatoes onto his plate.

"But you must tell us about it." Lottie coaxed. "The dead woman was one of those women at the Silver Window, wasn't she?"

"You seem to have all the details."

"Was she from that bawdy house or not?" Therese asked.

"She was." He answered. "And before any of you get any ideas about snooping around, let me remind you that crime investigation is police business."

"Surely you haven't forgotten all the help we've given you in the past." Lottie said.

"Yes and a great deal of trouble, as well." Charles responded.

"That's unfair." Sarah said.

"No it is not. Last time Chief Dolan was ready to fire me over what he called your *silly spinster shenanigans*."

"The nerve of that man!" Lottie said. "Everyone in town knows he's as lazy as the day is long."

"Maybe so, but the five of you just can't interfere in police work whenever you feel like it." Charles said.

"Look," Benjamin said. "If you don't want any help from us, then we won't help. Still it doesn't mean you can't share information with us. We might have some ideas."

Charles looked from one eager face to the next. "Okay, but you've got to promise to stay out of the investigation."

They nodded agreement. Charles knew from long experience just how long that promise would hold.

"Any clues?" Benjamin asked, hopefully.

"Not much. There was a silver flask nearby that the Chief believes was stolen from Maude Banning."

"Stolen my foot," Sarah said. "Maude Banning may have dropped it after she killed that woman."

"Without knowing the facts, that's a mighty big jump to a conclusion," Benjamin said. "The thing could have been out there for months…years even."

Charles nodded silently. He would not mention the earring for now. Police work could be dangerous; if they were going to play at solving this case, he wasn't going to make it easy for them.

"The flask isn't much." Benjamin mused. "But I've solved cases with less. There was this man in Boston…Must have been in '42, no. No it was earlier than that. I was new to the force. He thought he had gotten away with killing his wife and—"

"I'm sure you were good at what you did. Leastwise, you're always telling us that you were." Sarah said dismissively.

"Most likely it was one of her enemies." Agnes said. "But we can sort it out and—"

"This isn't a game." Charles admonished them. "Whoever killed this poor woman is dangerous. It wouldn't be prudent for any of you to start snooping around after him. The police force is capable of solving crimes."

"You've already said that we can offer you some unofficial help if we promise not to do anything dangerous."

All eyes were on Charles. They would help regardless of what he said. He knew this as well as they did. His agreement was merely a formality.

"Well--I suppose, if you share whatever suspicions you have with me and not go chasing after a killer on you own." Charles sighed.

They nodded silent agreement.

"In that case," Charles said. "I'll share one more thing with you---Chief Dolan wants me to speak with Maude Banning at the Silver Window tomorrow."

Six

A tall scowling woman opened the door. "Yes, what is it?" She asked.

Charles doffed his hat and explained the purpose of his visit.

"Chief Dolan is the one that comes to us when there is trouble." She snapped, slowly closing the door.

Charles' foot prevented her from completing the task.

"This time he sent me."

She opened the door and led him into a lavishly decorated parlor. "We all *like* Chief Dolan." She scowled. "I'll get Maude for you."

Underfoot was what Charles supposed to be an expensive floral carpet in shades of bright reds, purples, yellows and greens. Snow white Belgian lace curtains and thick red velvet drapes hung at the windows. The walls were covered in red velvet and gold foil brocade wallpaper, and were further adorned by several paintings of plump and inviting women in various stages of undress, cavorting or reclining in lush garden settings. Ornate gilt frames encased each work of art. A piano stood in one corner of the room, in another was a whatnot shelf filled with sparkling crystal cherubs. Placed nearby so that they might catch the warmth of the fireplace were two bottle green velvet wing chairs. Brass cuspidors were placed around the room. This was a parlor meant for a man to forget the cares of the day.

She strode silently into the room and extended a fleshy pink hand. "Rose tells me you want to see me."

"I'm Charles Bowling, Miss Banning." He said taking the proffered hand. "Special Assistant to Chief Bowling, I've come regarding an investigation."

. She sat on the settee and motioned him to be seated as well. "So, what can I do for you Mr. Bowling?"

"You've heard about the death of Mary Hanlon?" He asked.

"Yes, such a terrible thing."

He nodded in agreement. "She lived here?"

"No she didn't."

"No?"

"She was living elsewhere when she was murdered." Maude explained dabbing at the red curls piled high upon her head.

"Do you know why she was out in Six Mile Canyon?"

"I don't know why she would do anything. We had to let her go and that was the last we saw of her."

"Let her go?"

"Mary's drinking was a problem....She was a mean drunk. When she first came here she was so lovely...a favorite with all the men. Then she started drinking heavily. That and the laudanum ruined her looks and cheery disposition. There was no other choice."

"Do you know of anyone who might have killed her?"

Maude relaxed. Contemplating the gold rings on her fingers, she said. "Actually no Mr. Bowling, I can't imagine anyone wanting to kill Mary. I've already told you what a nasty temper she had when she'd had too much to drink, but it was certainly nothing worth killing her over."

He pulled the earring from his pocket and held it in his palm. "Have you ever seen this earring?"

She bent and stared at it. Something flickered behind her eyes. Was it recognition or fear? He couldn't be sure. Guardedly, she said. "I pay little attention to other women's jewelry. Why do you ask?"

"I believe it belonged to the dead woman."

Maude shuddered. "Ghastly. No I've never seen it."

An Asian man crept into the parlor. Carefully depositing an armload of logs into the fireplace, he lit the fire and hovered nearby until it was blazing.

"Will there be anything else Maude?" He asked.

"That will be all Wing Li."

Charles waited until the man bowed his way out of the parlor before asking, "Did Mary Hanlon have any family that you know of?" He asked.

"She talked of a sister in Carson City, but I don't know her name. From what I gathered, they were estranged, and had been for quite some time. She was friendly with the other girls, but not overly. Except for Bridget. Those two were thick as thieves there for a while consulting the spirits. They would get that thing they called a dial and claim to be talking with Bridget's dead sister and Mary's dead parents and George Washington if you can believe that." She laughed. "Such silliness, but then there is so little to occupy their minds. Talking with the spirits indeed."

Charles nodded agreement. Consulting the spirits was a pastime shared by many people in Virginia City. It seemed that every week a séance or Spiritualist meeting was being held somewhere in town. Just as often a famed spiritualist would come to town and lecture on the subject at Piper's Opera House. He'd read discourses on the subject and attended Lucinda Lloyd's lectures. His own beliefs on the matter remained simple and fixed. The dead are dead; as such, their communicating days are behind them.

"Why did the friendship end?" He asked abruptly.

"Mr. Bowling, I don't generally pay much attention to the girls' petty squabbles, someone is always upset with someone else. I suppose that since Louise and Bridget were closer in age they became good friends. That left Mary out in the cold." She frowned. "How dreadful for her to be murdered like that...I hope it had nothing to do with her spirit communications."

"Why do you say that?"

"It was merely a thought." She said.

"Have you ever attempted to contact anyone on the other side?"

She laughed loudly. "That Mrs. Loyd, up the road

claims to receive messages from the dead. But I have enough problems with those on this side. That dial nearly consumed Mary and Bridget. Mary would receive a message and Bridget was all ears. I often thought she was doing it just to get attention.

One night they came in here in front of the other girls and announced that the dial had predicted death for someone in the house. That is when I decided it was time put a stop to this so-called spirit communication of theirs. I had Wing Li throw the thing out of the house that very night. They were scaring the other girls half to death. After that nonsense I forbade anybody to talk of spirits and such in the house." She gazed out the window. "Now it seems, it was an accurate prediction after all."

"How did Mary Hanlon react?"

Maude's chubby fingers twisted the flashing bracelets that encircled her wrists. She examined the gold ring on her small finger and said, "She was very upset and threatened to leave. The mutinous little devil tried to incite the others to leave with her." Maude chuckled.

"After thinking about it awhile, I suppose she realized that no one else would put up with her shenanigans the way we did." She was suddenly pensive. "Mary was moody. Her temper tantrums put all the girls on edge. We tried to overlook her failings, but there were just too many of them. The Silver Window is a business after all."

The tall grandfather clock in the hall chimed loudly. Maude jumped to her feet. "I'm sorry. I have an appointment Mr. Bowling. If you have any more questions I will have to answer them some other time."

He wouldn't learn anything more from Maude Banning today.

Seven

Charles hitched his horse to the post in front of Mrs. Lloyd's brightly painted little house. Its front porch offered a direct view of the Silver Terrace Cemetery. Few people would appreciate such a view. But then most people didn't claim to communicate with the dead on a regular basis either.

As one of several seers and Spiritualists living in Virginia City Mrs. Lloyd earned her living telling fortunes and giving lectures on the subject of spirit communication. It was a career that women with no other options, took for themselves. Like the others, Mrs. Lloyd also added to her income by conducting séances for those wishing to continue meaningful dialog with their dearly departed. Occasionally a brave soul wanted her to look deep into her crystal ball and see what the future held. And this, she gladly did, for a fee.

Mrs. Lloyd opened her door with a hopeful, "Did you need me to tell your fortune sir?"

"No Mam. My name is Charles Bowling, Special

Assistant to Chief Dolan. I'd like to ask you some questions concerning spirit communication."

"Very well," she sighed. "Come in."

He raked his boots on the porch and stepped into one of the tiniest parlors he had ever seen, barely big enough for a settee and a chair. Mrs. Lloyd perched on the settee and said. "Please sit."

He did so.

"Now, before you commence asking me your questions I want you to understand that I charge a consulting fee."

"How much is that Mam?" He asked.

She thought a moment. "One dollar if your questions don't take up more than an hour of my time."

"That sounds reasonable to me." Charles said pulling a silver dollar from his pocket.

With her money firmly in hand, Mrs. Lloyd smiled and asked. "So what is it you want to know?"

"Have you heard about the murder in Six Mile Canyon?"

She nodded. "Considering the lifestyle, we shouldn't be surprised when one of these soiled doves is murdered."

"Yes." Charles agreed, though he had long ago stopped being shocked at the cruelty mankind is capable of. "The woman who was killed, Mary Hanlon, used the dial on occasion and I wondered if perhaps you might have been acquainted with her."

She eyed him coldly. "No I was not. There are other seers in town."

"Of course there are. But I've heard that you are

one of the best in Virginia City." He said. *Vanity thy name is woman.*

"Be that as it may, I never met the woman. I suggest you speak with my friend Edwina Darlington at the tailor shop near the Divide."

"Thank you, I'll do that. Do you believe it's possible to predict a death?"

"Well I, I, yes I believe it is. Even so, it certainly would not be proper for one to tell a client that his death was imminent. Although I've heard that the foolish Bowers woman has done that on occasion."

Charles nodded agreement. "Do you conduct private séances?"

"Yes of course I do. Not everyone wishes such matters discussed in public."

"I may wish to have you conduct a private séance at my residence in the very near future."

"You will find that my fees are quite reasonable." This so in case he labored under the misconception that such service was free.

"Oh I am sure." He smiled.

Mrs. Lloyd beamed. In her estimation Charles's importance had just risen. No longer a mere interrogator, he was now a customer. "In that case I shall be delighted to conduct your séance Mr. Bowling." She shivered and stood. "These Washoe Zephyrs, they whistle their way through the walls and right up through the floorboards. Would you like coffee?"

"No thank you, Mrs. Lloyd. I'll be on my way for now."

She followed him out onto the front porch, where the wind whipped loose greying strands of her matronly rolled and plaited hairdo.

"My, what a handsome bay," she said gazing at Charles horse. "I rode every day as a girl. Bays and sorrels were always my favorites." She said wistfully.

He acknowledged the compliment to his horse with a smile. And as he rode back to town he tried to imagine Mrs. Lloyd as a young horsewoman.

Eight

Lottie and Agnes liked to keep busy. In addition to the Ducks and Deeks, they owned the Comstock book store with Sarah, and volunteered at the Virginia City Charitable Society.

In a backroom office of Reverend Anderson, members of the society took in donations of clothing and canned goods for the needy of their city. Women who suddenly found themselves widowed by mining accidents had a place to turn to for help in feeding and clothing their children. What the Miners' Union could not provide the Charitable Society did, even if that help meant only a willing ear or a shoulder to cry on.

On this morning Lottie and Agnes were the only two who braved the raging winds to receive the day's donations. As the morning crept on with no one coming to the door, Agnes began pacing the floor nervously; she spotted a broom in the corner and grabbed it, giving the floor a quick sweeping.

The task finished, she said. "I'm going over and see how Sarah is doing in the bookstore."

No sooner had she left than a pretty young woman walked in with a bundle of clothing.

Blushing, the raven-haired beauty stammered. "I am so very sorry. You see, Mrs. Waters asked me to deliver these to you shortly before she left.... and with the death of Mr. Eldons I completely forgot."

Lottie smiled sympathetically. "You must be Hannah, the caretaker Miriam raves about."

The woman blushed again. "Yes."

Lottie took the clothing from her. "Never you mind. As far as I'm concerned this donation came in the day Miriam's stage left town."

Hannah smiled gratefully. "Thank you so much you are most kind Mrs.--"

"Mrs. Duckworth." Lottie smiled.

"Pleased to meet you," Hannah said extending a slender hand.

Lottie took the girl's hand in hers. "My pleasure dear. Please thank Mrs. Waters for her generosity."

. "Yes mam I will." She glanced at the old clock that hung near the window. "Oh, I must be running along. Thank you again Mrs. Duckworth."

"Wait just a moment Hannah." Lottie said.

The girl stopped and turned slowly toward her. "Yes Mrs. Duckworth?"

"Have you heard any word on when Mrs. Waters, might be returning?"

Hannah's face tightened. "She is expected at month's end."

No wonder she had scampered out in weather like this with the donation.

Lottie smiled. "I'm sure Mr. Waters is delighted."

"Oh yes that he is."

Lottie thanked her again and was stacking the dresses in a pile when Agnes returned.

"Finally received a donation did we?" She asked, reaching for a tan and black stripped dress. "This looks like one of Miriam's day frocks."

"Her housekeeper just brought them in." Lottie said.

"The young lady I passed at the door?" Agnes

asked.

Lottie nodded. "And dear, she told me that Miriam is set to return at the end of the month."

Agnes clapped her hands together happily. "Oh Lottie, that's wonderful news." She examined the striped dress closely. "And when she does return, I shall ask her why she donated this dress without first repairing the underarm seams or replacing the missing buttons."

They laughed merrily at the thought.

Agnes suddenly stopped laughing. "Still it is very odd."

"What is that?" Lottie asked.

"This dress—it's one of Miriam's favorites, and strange that she would give it away."

"Perhaps she was tired of it." Lottie said.

"Perhaps." Agnes answered.

Nine

Jack Murphy's Saloon was situated nearest the Silver Window and the rail station. If any place might yield information, Charles reasoned, it was that place. He stepped inside and the smell of stale beer assaulted his nose. As his eyes adjusted to the saloon's cavernous darkness, he noticed several miners standing at the bar, a card game was being played in the corner, and to his relief the piano stood silent.

"What can I get you, mister?"

Charles ordered a beer, introduced himself and said, "I'm looking into the murder out in the canyon."

"Too much killing going on if you ask me," the bartender said. "You talking about that Mary Hanlon getting herself killed?"

"I am. Charles said. "Did she come in here?"

"Good God no!" The bartender said slapping the overflowing glass on the bar.

"Those women over in the houses keep to themselves. But her husband, he used to come in all the time, and cry in his beer 'bout how wrong she'd done him. Nice fellow. He was crazy about her, but she just couldn't stop drinking. Said he was getting tired of her being drunk all the time and he would put her out of the house one day."

Charles downed the beer. "When do you expect he might be back in?"

The bartender chuckled. "Wellsir, I reckon he won't be coming back this way anytime soon. He was killed in that big cave in at the Kentuck last spring."

With his suspect dead and buried months before the killing occurred, Charles saw no need to linger, "A woman like Mary Hanlon probably had enemies." He said absently.

"'Course she did." The bartender said. "The woman was just plain no good."

"You knew her then?"

"No, not except for what her husband said about her. Get you another?"

"One is sufficient." Charles answered.

The bartender yanked a towel from his back pocket and absently wiped the bar. He had nothing more to say to Charles.

Ten

With the murder of Mary Hanlon an air of excitement had returned to Ducks and Deeks. At dinner they all gathered around Charles, hoping to gain knowledge that might help them to help him.

He ate in silence and looked from one face to the other. These were his family, his friends. They were all good people who'd lived long productive lives, except for Therese of course who'd barely hit twenty. What did it hurt to share a few bits of information with them, he asked himself.

"As long as you remember that you are not to go chasing after a killer—"

He began by telling them about his trip to the brothel and to the saloon. They listened intently as he shared his opinion of the articulate and obviously well-educated Maude, the parlor's décor, and Mary Hanlon's having delved into the spirit world. When he was finished Lottie asked. "Do you believe someone at the Silver Window murdered her?"

Charles shook his head. "Any of them could have I suppose."

Lottie said. "I know the Spiritualism is all the rage at the moment. But it still seems odd to me that those women were all up there playing with a dial and attempting to consult the dead."

"Plotting murder is more like it." Agnes sniffed.

"There is nothing wrong with Spiritualism. Many people are interested in the spirit world." Sarah said.

"I don't necessarily agree that it's possible to contact the dead, but it does give pause for thought."

"I wonder how many of them see a death predicted." Therese shuddered. "That would stop me from ever indulging in such things."

Charles smiled. "These women weren't that wise Therese."

"I don't think wisdom had anything to do with it." She said.

"I read in the morning paper that Lucinda Lloyd is giving another lecture on spirit communication tomorrow night at Piper's. We should go." Agnes said.

"Oh Agnes! What a splendid idea." Lottie said. "We might learn something that will help us in our investigation."

Charles and Benjamin moved to a corner of the parlor and lit their cigars. They puffed contentedly. Finally Benjamin said, "Their investigation, humph."

Charles laughed.

"I don't think that contraption had anything to do with the murder." Benjamin said.

"Neither do I."

Benjamin tapped his ash in the brass cuspidor and said,

"In fact, I'm wondering if Maude told you that story to throw you off the trail."

"That's possible." Charles agreed. He stubbed his cigar out. "Martin Harris has asked that I meet him in his office tomorrow."

"That young man is an ass whose ambition knows

no bounds."

"I won't deny that. He's already making noises about wanting the case solved quickly."

Eleven

Storey County District Attorney Martin Harris greeted Charles with a warm smile and a firm handshake. "Have a seat." He waved toward the straight back chair that sat opposite his desk.

"How are we coming on this murder investigation?" Martin asked.

The memory of John Millian's execution for the murder of prostitute Julia Bulette was still fresh in everyone's mind. Before it faded entirely, he wanted a trial that would showcase his oration skill. It must be something that would capture the entire county's attention and that of Carson City as well. Perhaps another public execution would gain him the political attention he craved.

Charles glanced around the office, strangely empty without the former District Attorney's prized leather bound tomes. "Well we've only begun—so there is nothing new I'm afraid." Charles sighed. Disappointment registered on Martin's face. "They weren't able tell you anything at the Silver Window?"

"What they told me was not very helpful."

Martin nervously flipped the pages of the book he had been reading. "I didn't get to be the youngest District Attorney ever elected in Storey County by not sending criminals to prison---or the gallows when necessary." He closed the book. "Chief Dolan has assured me that this case will be solved quickly. You recall how this town reacted when Julia Bulette was killed?"

"I've not seen that same outrage with this victim." Charles said.

"Of course not, man! Bulette was murdered in her own bed. A stone's throw from the police department, that's enough to scare the bejesus out of folks. This Hanlon creature deserves justice too. And by God, I mean to see that she gets it."

"As do I," Charles assured him.

Mollified, Martin leaned across the desk. "I've been meaning to ask you something about Chief Dolan. "Would you agree with me that he is getting up there?"

Charles flinched. If Martin was attempting to shove the chief out to pasture he would have to find someone else to help him do it. "No I would not agree with you at all."

Martin's expression changed, as Charles continued. "Chief Dolan is highly regarded because he runs an effective department."

A slow smile spread across Martin's face. "That doesn't mean he isn't an old man well past his prime. But yes, I like that. Loyalty, it's an admirable trait, Charles."

Twelve

At the Miners Union Hall a balding little man pushed papers around on an otherwise tidy desk. When the bell on the door rang, he looked up curiously. "What can I do for you?"

Charles introduced himself and said, "I'm looking for information on a man by the name of Joseph Hanlon. I'm told he was killed in a cave in at the Kentuck last year."

The man opened a drawer of a cabinet. Thumbing through papers he said, "Name doesn't sound familiar. What did he do?"

"He was a miner."

Grimacing at Charles' ignorance, the clerk fished out a sheet of paper. "Yup. He was working at the Kentuck all right…But he didn't die in the cave in."

"Oh? So how did he die?"

"According to this information Mr. Hanlon was fired for smoking in the mine. Took his days' wage and that was the last we saw of him."

"How many days was that before the big cave-in?" Charles asked.

"He was fired on the 19th and the cave in occurred on the. ---Well I'll be damned." He said staring at the paper. "The cave in occurred on the very same day. How's that for luck? If not for his firing, he might have been dead himself."

"Do you happen to have his last address?"

"He roomed at the Morrow House."

The Morrow House sat too near the infamous Barbary Coast to be considered truly elegant. Its roomers were mostly single businessmen, new in town and hoping to strike it rich at one of the silver mines. After a few questions Charles learned that none of them knew, or remembered Joseph Hanlon. The owner had recently acquired the property and quickly informed him that the woman he wanted to talk with was buried at the Gold Hill Cemetery.

"Doubtful you'll get much help there." She grinned.

He resisted the urge to tell her about the work that Spiritualists like Mrs. Lloyd and Mrs. Darlington were engaged in. She walked him out the front door and down the steps to the hitching post. "Sorry I couldn't have helped you more." She smiled shyly and turned back toward the house.

Charles reined the horse, ready to head down the hill when a young blonde woman scampered out the door calling, "Wait a minute there mister. Hold up."

He stopped and waited.

"They just told me you was asking about Joseph."

"Did you know him?" Charles asked hopefully.

"Yes." She said. "At one time we was, we was--" She blushed. "We was what you might call right friendly."

"When did he die?"

She giggled. "That's what he had us tell those he owed money to--and his missus. But he's no more dead than you and me. He just wanted to make a new start is all." She boasted.

"It's very important that I speak with him. Where is he?"

"Not tellin' if you're gonna put him in jail." She said suddenly distrustful.

"He won't go to jail unless he killed his wife."

She relaxed. "Joseph's no killer. He'll tell you hisself. Go on down to thirty one G. Street. He lives there with my brother."

"And you are--?"

"Dora, my name's Dora." She grinned, happy and toothless.

The shack on G. Street was so dilapidated a good windstorm would tear it to shreds. At his knock a skinny young man opened the front door, smiling broadly. Rotten teeth must run in the family, Charles thought staring at the man's black stumps of teeth.

"Dora told me I'd find Joseph Hanlon here."

"That a fact? Well just who the hell are you mister?" The young man asked, still smiling.

"I'm Charles Bowling, Special assistant to Police Chief Dolan."

"Okay, c'mon in."

Charles stepped into unimaginable squalor. The house was as close to a pigsty as he ever wanted to get. Old newspapers, empty cans and beer bottles were scattered throughout the parlor and cobwebs hung in the corners. In the kitchen a stack of dirty dishes and filthy linens covered the sinks and the stove. Stepping over the filth, he wondered how anyone could live like this.

Joseph Hanlon was at the table eating a cold biscuit. He eyed Charles warily. "I've done nothing wrong, mister."

Charles pulled out a stool and carefully brushed away crumbs and dust. Satisfied that the stool was reasonably clean, he sat down. " I'm trying to understand why you allowed your wife to believe you were dead?"

"Aint no law against that besides, I had my reasons."

"Why not just divorce her?"

"Ever lived with a drunk?" He asked looking Charles up and down. "No I guess you haven't. I just needed to get away from Mary and her drinking." He explained.

"I've been told that your wife had a sister in Carson City. Do you happen to know her name?"

Hanlon threw his head back and laughed wildly. "She'll be nothing but a waste of time for you. That fine lady wouldn't have nothing to do with Mary when she was alive. She aint gonna want anything to do with her now that she's dead."

"I asked you for her name." Charles reminded him firmly.

"Name's Mrs. John Bramwell," Hanlon spat. "Her husband's part of those rich Bramwells with their fine mansion and all their lumber and such."

"I see." Charles said.
"Do you know why she and Mary were estranged?" Charles asked.

Hanlon shrugged. "I don't rightly know. Whatever it was happened long before I met Mary."

"How long were the two of you married?"

"'Bout ten years. Long enough for me I tell you."

"I've heard that you used to frequent Jack Murphy's Saloon and cry in your drink over Mary." Charles taunted.

Hanlon grinned. "Yeah I used to feel pretty bad about her drinking up all the money. Was crazy for love of her till I met--till I met Dora."

Remembering the toothless Dora, Charles shuddered inwardly. There's no accounting, he decided. "As a matter of fact the folks at Jack Murphy's still think you're dead. So do a few others in town."

Hanlon laughed. "That's all right by me."

"Where were you when your wife was murdered?" Charles asked gazing at the other man's hands.

"I was nowhere near her I can tell you that, mister. Most likely I was right here playing cards with my friends. You can ask 'em if you like."

Dora's brother broke his silence. "That's so mister! Joseph, he was here all night just like he says."

"And what night was that?" Charles asked him.

The man shrugged his shoulders. "I don't rightly know. What night was it Joseph?"

"Anyone else vouch for you?"

"Couple others were here that night." Hanlon said. "I reckon they'll tell you."

"Why didn't you come forward when you realized

that your wife was seeking work at the Silver Window?"

"Why should I?" He shrugged. "Mary was a drunk. You couldn't do anything with her. Once she thought I was dead and the money wasn't coming in regularly she did what she could to keep herself in liquor."

Charles asked. "Can you think of anyone who might have had reason to kill her?"

"Can't think of a soul, except me." Hanlon laughed.

"Is that so?" Charles asked coldly.

"I wasted too many good years of my life on her." Hanlon explained. "And she turned out to be nothing but a drunk." He took the last bite of his biscuit. "I didn't love her anymore no how. Why should I care if she's dead? No account drunk."

"That may be." Charles said. "But she didn't deserve to die like she did."

Hanlon studied him intently. "I reckon not."

Thirteen

Sarah pulled the ribbons of her cape and looked around the crowded opera house. She'd forgotten how much she enjoyed attending an event at Piper's.

"I am so glad you persuaded me to come." She said, giving Therese's hand a warm squeeze.

At that moment, Martin Harris, the newly elected

Storey County District Attorney, resplendent in his elegant evening attire recognized them. "Mrs. Duckworth, Mrs. Deeks, Miss Browne and Mr. Thorndale how nice to see you. You are looking very lovely this evening ladies" He said, his eyes on Therese. "Therese, it is a most pleasant surprise to see you. I thought I would have to sit alone." He smiled at her. "May I sit on your other side?"

"Please do Martin." Therese said.

Agnes glanced around the opera house feeling very fashionable and smart in her new dress and black velvet hat trimmed with white feathers. No one had a hat nearly as splendid. Obviously that new bottle green color was very popular this year. Nearly every woman was wearing the shade tonight. It was an intriguing color, but she preferred black, as it didn't give the skin that sallow appearance that green shades often did. She smirked at the thought of so many women adhering to the dictates of fashion even to their own detriment.

She thought of Mary Hanlon and glanced at the boxes where the ladies of the evening were expected to sit during all performances. Shrouded behind gauze they, and the decent citizenry, were protected from the curious gazes of the other. Movement drew her eyes away from the boxes. There was something oddly familiar about the person she stared at. She reached for her opera glasses to get a better look. A burly man in evening attire stepped into her field of vision, preventing her from doing so. But yes, she had seen that face before. Now if she could only remember where she'd seen it. Before she had time to ponder the question further the curtain rose on the empty stage and a hush fell across Piper's Opera House.

Fourteen

Mort Coombs and his wife lived in a shack at the edge of Chinatown. The elderly couple spent their days in the canyons foraging for jackrabbits and gathering the sticks of firewood that the Chinese wood gatherers missed. The hapless rabbits were skinned for their soft fur, and then tossed into the stew pot.

Firewood was a rare commodity on Mt. Davidson; the few dollars the Coombs earned from the sale of their wood provided them with a stake in the regular evening card games.

The proximity of Mort's shack to the Six Mile Canyon Road had roused Charles' curiosity on the day Mary Hanlon's body was discovered. Rather than attend the Spiritualist lecture at Piper's he rode down to Mort's.

Smoke spiraled from the chimney, and a lantern blazed in the window. The day's haul of stove wood must have been meager. Without money for the card game, the old couple stayed home. Charles dismounted and knocked at the door of the shack. Eyeing him curiously, Mort swung the door open wide. Beside him, a large dog barked menacingly.

"Hush up Pedro!" He commanded. "Why Charlie, what can I do for you?"

A low growl rose up in Pedro's throat. Mort smacked the dog lightly. "You don't hush I'm gonna put you outdoors and let the coyotes get you." He threatened. The dog was silent.

"You gonna be so rude as to not invite him in?" Mort's wife admonished stepping from behind her husband.

Mort stepped aside. "'Course not. C'mon in Charlie."

Charles tipped his hat to the old woman and stepped into the shack. Pedro eyed him curiously. Two rickety chairs were pulled up to a wooden box near the wood stove, a pile of worn feather pillows and faded rags in the corner was the pallet where they slept. Mort offered Charles one of the chairs and he and his wife plopped onto their bed.

"Pedro, come here." She said. The dog ran to her and curled up on the pallet beside her.

"I'm sorry to disturb you."

"We weren't doing anything 'cept talking." Mort said

"Where's my manners?" Mrs. Coombs asked slowly raising herself from the pallet. "Care for a cup of coffee, Charlie?"

"No thank you Mam."

She eased back onto the pallet and absently ran her fingers through her long gray hair.

Charles had known the old couple since he was a boy. Then they had lived in a large mansion up on B.

Street with the finest furnishings, several servants and a custom designed maroon carriage, trimmed in silver, at their disposal. Two of the Comstock's first millionaires, they'd struck it rich near Gold Canyon while other miners were still foolishly toiling at the northern edge of town.

Both had come from poor immigrant families, neither was literate or worldly. All their wealth could not buy them prestige, or the respect and friendship of the town's educated citizens who envied them their money and mocked them behind their backs.

Instead of helping their cause, the generous donations the Coombs had given to the Fireman's fund, the miners' union and the church benevolent societies only intensified that envy.

Lonely and friendless, they turned to gambling. Unlike other citizens of the Comstock, the card players at the local card games welcomed the Coombs and their cash with open arms. They became regulars. In time they lost everything, the mansion, the coach and the mine. And still they gambled.

"It's about that woman who was killed in the canyon the other night." Charles said.

"Good God, Charlie! We don't know nothing about no murder."

Mrs. Coombs pushed a strand of wiry gray hair from her eyes. "You know us. We keep to ourselves, and don't get mixed up in other folks troubles."

"'And we damn sure aint murderers."

Mrs. Coombs gasped. "You will kindly watch your tongue, Mortimer Coombs." She admonished.

Charles smiled broadly. They might be unlucky and unworldly, but they certainly weren't anyone he would ever suspect of murder.

"I wanted to ask you if you happened to see anything out of the ordinary that night. Anything you can think of might help catch this killer."

Mort scratched his head. "Nah we don't know nothing."

"Are you sure?"

"'Course I am. Nothing ever happens round here."

Charles stood to leave. He'd long ago resigned himself to the fact that not all hunches paid off. If he hurried he just might be able to meet Therese and the others at Piper's.

"Now…wait a minute. Just a minute. I do remember something." Mort said.

"We'd just come back from a card game at old man Garner's place. The missus she went on inside on account of it was cold and the wind was blowing. The wind sometimes bothers her throat, it's kinda delicate, you understand?"

Charles nodded his understanding of Mrs. Coombs' delicate throat and the old man continued.

"I stayed outdoors to watch the moon, it was right pretty that night all full it was. Kinda moon me and the missus used to---" He patted his wife's hand tenderly. "When we was young we sometimes would sit outdoors most of the night gazing up at the full moon." He said lost in his memories.

"Go on with you Mort. Charlie don't want to hear none of that." Mrs. Coombs laughed.

"About the other night," Charles coaxed.

"I was fixing to go inside when I see this buggy coming up outta the canyon road like the devil hisself was chasing after it. The missus she came out about that same time to tell me to come on in. It was getting late. Two people was riding in that buggy. I heard one of them screaming 'You made a murderer of me twice!' Then the other said. 'Afore long we will be allright.' That was alls we heard. "

Charles looked at Mrs. Coombs. "You heard the same thing?"

"I heard someone screaming…Sounded like Chinese to me. I couldn't make out what they was saying."

"Her hearing aint what it used to be," Mort explained.

Mrs. Coombs glared at her husband. "My hearing's just fine Mortimer! I say they was talking Chinese."

"Would you know the voices if you heard them again?"

"Nah Charlie," Mort laughed. "It was just two people, that's about all I could tell you."

"Could you tell if they were men or women?"

"I don't rightly know. But I'm guessing it was two men." Mort said.

"Two Chinese men," Mrs. Coombs added, "I know what I heard."

Charles thanked the old couple for their time and headed back up the hill.

Fifteen

On Sunday the women went to church, leaving Charles and Benjamin in the parlor with the newspaper and their cigars.

They cut and lit their cigars in silence. After a few puffs Charles said, "I spoke with Joseph Hanlon yesterday. The man lives in a filthy rat's nest."

"I thought he was killed in the cave in at the Kentuck." Benjamin said.

"So did his wife. He gave me the name of Mary Hanlon's sister in Carson City. Mrs. John Bramwell, can you believe that? I'll need to go down and talk to her."

"If she'll even speak with you," Benjamin said.

"She will."

"Might I offer you some advice? Benjamin asked. Charles nodded assent and he continued. "The wealthy are very guarded in matters such as this. Take Therese with you. A woman is likely to feel more at ease and share a lot more things with another woman than she will a man. Having a woman along also makes your official visit more palatable to the servants and the neighbors."

Charles saw the wisdom of Benjamin's words. "Yes, that's a very good idea." He agreed.

"So Hanlon, given that he is alive, do you suppose he killed his wife?

"Joseph Hanlon is the type that would kill his own

mother if he saw benefit." Charles answered. "That said, I don't think he is our murderer. But I'm not ready to discard the possibility just yet."

"We're certainly not without some cut throat characters. Everything Maude Banning told you up at the bawdy house is humbug." Benjamin said, placing his cigar in the ashtray.

Charles nodded and continued enjoying his cigar.

The room was silent except for the mantle clock with its pendulum that rhythmically ticked away the minutes. Benjamin had nodded off. Charles settled back on the circular sofa. Why, he wondered, would Maude try to throw him off the track—unless she knew exactly how and why Mary Hanlon met her death.

Sixteen

The moon hung low in the western sky. Charles and Therese headed south toward Gold Hill, Silver City and on to Carson City. As the horses galloped across the Divide the ensuing breeze stirred up dust and pebbles. Therese wrapped her blue woolen cape tightly around her shoulders and edged closer to Charles. Until sun up the journey through the Divide would be a very cold one. They rode in companionable silence, broken only by the buggy's wheels and the steady clip clop of the horses' hooves.

As they crossed between the tall jutting rocks that form Devil's Gate, Therese finally spoke. "I cannot even imagine a sister turning her back on her own sister." She stared into the distance. "What do you suppose she will be like?"

"I haven't given much thought to that."

Therese laughed. "Well I have. Ever since you invited me to come along I have tried to picture her in my mind."

"I'm sure she is markedly different than her sister." Charles said.

Therese laughed. "That's a given. But after interviewing her we'll either be able to scratch her off our suspect list or focus more attention on her."

"We," he stressed, "have no suspect list or attention to focus."

"You could easily have asked any of the others to accompany you today, but you asked for *my* help.

And you shall get it." Therese reminded him.
Charles smiled broadly. "And so I did."

They arrived in Carson City around noon. The street was far wider than any of those on the Comstock, and not nearly so muddy, even with the recent rains. Here and there a tree stood alongside the street near elegant false front buildings. The city was situated in a valley of rich farmland, kept green by the nearby Carson River.

To the west the snowcapped Sierra Nevada Mountains rose like sentinels. There were no mines operating every hour of the day and night, here. Consequently, Carson City was quieter than Virginia City, even though state's politicians headquartered here.

The Bramwell mansion was less than a block from Carson Street, situated where two narrow streets converged. The two-story home, like many in the city, was built of gray brown sandstone blocks, quarried nearby. "I've seen miners' cabins smaller than this front porch." Charles remarked as he rang the brass bell.

A woman in black dress, white apron and cap answered the door. "Yes?" She asked, eyeing Charles and Therese suspiciously.

"Good afternoon. I am Charles Bowling, special assistant to Virginia City's Chief of Police Dolan and this is my assistant Miss Gunderson." Charles said, handing her his calling card. "We would like a word with Mrs. Bramwell."

"Very well." She led them through a hallway carpeted in expensive Brussels carpet, and into a small sitting room. "Wait here and I shall see if Mrs. Bramwell is available" She commanded.

The room's large bay windows were covered in cream-colored velvet drapes, parted so that the warm afternoon sunshine streamed in, lending an air of cheeriness.

Mrs. Bramwell entered the room scowling. The resemblance to her sister was uncanny.
. "Please have a seat." She said waving a tiny hand at a mauve velvet sofa.

When they were seated, Mrs. Bramwell perched ramrod straight on the sofa opposite them.

"You are with the Virginia City police?" She asked.

"Yes Mrs. Bramwell. I'm Charles Bowling and this is my assistant Miss Gunderson."

She acknowledged Therese with a nod and asked. "How may I help you?"

Charles said. "First let me inform you—"

"It concerns your sister, Mary." Therese broke in.

"I have nothing to say about her and don't wish to discuss her with you." Mrs. Bramwell said. "Now if you will excuse me."

"I am afraid it's not going to be that easy mam." Charles said. "You see, we are investigating your sister's murder."

"Murdered? Mary is dead?" She gasped. "Surely you don't think that I had anything to do with her death."

"Of course not." Therese lied. "We are simply trying to discover who might have had reason to kill her. Won't you help us?"

"We promise you that we shall be very discreet." Charles added.

Mrs. Bramwell sighed audibly and smiled at Therese. "It has been several years since I last saw Mary. I don't really see how I can be of any help to you. I--I always knew something like this would happen one day. She was almost without conscience. Other people's feelings meant nothing to her. Have you ever known someone like that?"

Therese nodded. "Yes, I have."

"When is the last time you heard from your sister?" Charles asked.

"She wrote to me regularly. But I tore up all the letters."

"May we ask what caused your estrangement?" Therese asked.

Mrs. Bramwell suddenly jumped up. "No you may not! It was a personal matter that has no bearing on your investigation!"

"I believe that I can best be the judge of that." Charles said.

Mrs. Bramwell turned to Therese. "I shall refer to it as sibling rivalry that got out of hand. "

"I see." Therese said calmly. "

"According to witnesses Mary spoke of you often." Charles said.

"We were strangers. I'm afraid I couldn't tell you what she did or didn't say."

Charles stood. "One or two more things before we

go Mrs. Bramwell. Have you ever participated in spirit communication, a séance for instance?"

"Certainly not!" She hissed. "The very idea is ludicrous."

"Would it surprise you to learn that your sister claimed to talk with spirits regularly?" Charles asked.

"As I've already told you, Mr. Bowling we were strangers."

"Were you acquainted with her husband, Joseph Hanlon?"

She gasped. "A thoroughly despicable man, he came here once and tried to extort money from me. To her credit, Mary put a stop to it. But now, now that she is dead---"

"I will see to it that he doesn't bother you again." Charles said.

.

The horses moved at a slow steady gait, as they drew the buggy up the side of the canyon. The night air was cold on Therese's face. Peering out from the hood of her cape, she stared at the sky dotted with stars.

"What are your thoughts on Mrs. Bramwell?" Charles asked.

"She may not appear to be the sort, but I would not be surprised if she had killed her sister."

She's certainly wealthy enough to have paid someone to do it--It's too sad to even think about."

"All such killings are." Charles reminded her.

She smiled. "I truly hope she had nothing to do with it. The murderer could be a miner that works out in the canyon."

"Who just happened upon her and murdered her for no good reason?" Charles asked incredulous.

"No. She might have discovered a secret silver lode."

"When did she do this?" Charles asked.

"I don't know, but it is possible."

"Anything is possible Therese."

Seventeen

The next morning Charles was back on Silver Window's front porch, with more questions.

Scowling, Rose opened the door. "Maude has gone out."

"I didn't come to see her." Charles said brushing past her. "I want to speak with the two women who befriended Mary Hanlon--Bridget and Louise."

She studied him intently. "They are working!"

Charles smiled. "That's okay. I'll wait."

"It'll be a long one. They will be working all night." She sneered.

"Perhaps I should go up and find them myself." He said, heading toward the stairway.

"That won't be necessary." She said. And then turning toward the hall, she called, "Wing Li!"

The houseman came running.

"Please show this--gentleman to the kitchen. And take Bridget and Louise to him when they are free."

Wing Li eyed Charles coldly. And bowing low he said, "Please follow me sir."

Roomy and warm, the kitchen was filled with the delicious aroma of onions and spices. Charles looked at the large kettle of beef stew bubbling on the stove and wondered how it compared to that of Mrs. Noonan. Certainly it smelled every bit as inviting. A plate of corn muffins and a stack of mismatched bowls perched precariously on a nearby counter. Unlike those who sold their favors on street corners, the women who worked here were not going hungry.

"Please have a seat." Wing Li offered waving toward the table.

Charles sat in a straight back chair. The room held nothing of the parlor's elegance and yet it was somehow more real and inviting.

"Care for a cup of tea while you wait?" Wing Li asked brusquely.

"No thanks."

"I will bring the ladies to you as soon as they are available." Another low bow and he was gone.

Charles gazed at a sampler that hung on the wall. Someone had carefully embroidered flowers and ribbons and the words *Home Sweet Home.* He sneezed. Once...twice...there must be cats in residence.

Wing Li walked silently into the kitchen took a wooden spoon from the cupboard and absently stirred the stew.

"Do you have many cats here?" Charles asked.

Wing Li contemplated him a moment. "Maybe six. We keep them because of the mice."

"Yes we also have problems with mice. "

"The ladies will be done soon." Wing Li assured him without a glance.

He put the spoon down, turned and dashed from the kitchen. He returned with two young women. The taller of the two was slender and rosy skinned, and stunningly beautiful. Her glossy dark hair hung in a neat thick plait. But it was her eyes that captivated Charles. Never in his life had he seen eyes the deep green color of hers. He stared into them so long that she laughed nervously. He glanced at the shorter woman, stocky with skin so fair it was nearly translucent. Her face was liberally sprinkled with large coppery freckles, and thick flaming red hair tumbled in a curly cascade down her back. Neither looked much older than some of the students Therese taught at the Second Ward School.

"Bridget and Louise." Wing Li announced and was gone.

The young women stared suspiciously at Charles. "Please be seated," he said pulling his notes from his coat pocket. The women sat at the table and eyed him curiously.

"I'm Charles Bowling assistant to Police Chief Dolan. I'm working on the investigation into the death of Mary Hanlon. Please forgive me, but I don't know which of you is which.'

The women smirked at each other.

"I am Bridget." The dark haired girl said nonchalantly, "and this is Louise." She waved a dainty hand at the redhead.

He smiled. "Let's start with you Bridget. I believe that you and Mary Hanlon were friends."

"Only for a short time."

"And why is that?"

"She was crazy."

"Did you and she use the dial to communicate with the spirit world?"

She threw back her head and laughed. "I knew it was nonsense! But Mary, she was so foolish about it. She truly believed that she was speaking with dead people."

"And who was she speaking with?"

She looked at Charles as if he'd suddenly lost his mind. "Mr. Bowling, do you seriously believe that you can talk to the dead?"

Louise giggled and his face turned crimson. Bridget was quick witted. Ignoring her question, he turned his attention to Louise and asked, "how well did you know Mary Hanlon?'

"Not so much. She, well--she and me, we didn't care for each other. She didn't like any of us, save Bridget. Mary, she was older than the rest of us and mayhap she didn't like it when the men quit wanting her."

He turned back to Bridget. "Have you any idea who might want to harm Mary?"

She shook her head. "I don't know who killed her. She might have been a mean drunk, but it's no reason to kill her."

"She had no enemies?" He asked incredulous.

"No sir, not a one."

Louise frowned. "But Bridget, you're forgetting that time she got in a fight with Sally Swan over the laudanum. Mary had this cough that sounded like a dog barking. She drank laudanum to quiet it some."

"She fought with someone?"

"She didn't have any more of her own so she stole Sally's laudanum. Sally was so mad she tried to scratch Mary's eyes out. Probably would have if Rose hadn't stepped between 'em."

"Sally said she'd slice Mary's throat open with her own sewing scissors if she ever went near her room again." Bridget added.

"Come to think of it, Mary lost her scissors shortly

after that. Mayhap Sally kept her promise." Louise said.

Charles saw no point in telling them that Mary had been strangled. "Where is Sally now?" He asked.

"Maude sent her packing when she got wind of the trouble. Last we seen her she was living in a crib over near Union Street." Louise said.

"But that's not the last time we heard of her. Don't you remember that gentlemen came by and told us she was working in one of those saloons up on the Barbary Coast?"

Louise remembered. "Said she was crazy as a bedbug...."

"Did she blame Mary for being ousted?"

"She went outta here kicking and screaming. Wing Li had to almost shove her out the door. Said she was coming back someday and fix Rose and Maude and Mary."

"Wing Li put her out?"

"He does Maude's bidding...And Rose's too."

Charles scribbled furiously on his crumpled sheet of paper knowing Martin Harris would eventually pour over the notes. "So Rose ordered Wing Li to throw Sally out?" He asked.

Both women nodded. "But she's strong too. She coulda done the job herself. I once saw her throw a man outta here by herself once." Louise offered.

"Did Mary ever have visitors other than customers?"

Bridget smiled. "There was one time this lady come up in a fine claret colored town coach, all fitted out with shiny brass. She and Mary talked on the porch awhile. Then all of a sudden they started yelling and clawing at each other."

"Did Mary say who the lady was?"

"No. She was covered by a veil like she didn't want anybody to see her."

"I think it was that sister she talked about." Louise suggested.

"Rose and Wing Li ran out there and pulled them apart. They sent the lady away in her fine coach and brought Mary inside. Rose screamed at her a long time, and Mary commenced to cry. I fell asleep listening to her."

Charles also wondered if the lady visitor had been Mrs. Bramwell. He said, "Okay. Let's talk about the dial again."

Bridget and Louise exchanged smiles.

"Do you recall what caused the two of you to stop using it?"

"It was the night the dial said that death was coming. We got so scared we decided to stop asking it questions. But then Rose told Maude and Maude took it away from Mary. Wing Li took it to the garbage."

"And that was the end of it? There was no more spirit communication?"

"Yes."

"No Bridget don't you remember when--" She caught herself.

"When what?" Charles coaxed.

She looked at Bridget then him. "Well it wasn't nothing. A few days before she left Mary came here in the kitchen and said the spirits were angry with

Rose on account of her telling Maude about the dial."

"Did she say how she knew this?"

Bridget jumped in. "Mary was a drunk. Sometimes she just said things that didn't make much sense."

Louise nodded agreement. "Mary didn't have good sense when she was drinking. The night she refused to go upstairs with that old man I saw Rose's face and I knew. I just knew they were going to send her packing."

Bridget smiled sadly. "Rose didn't care for her. When she got her chance she took it."

"So it was Rose' idea for Mary to go away?"

They nodded their heads.

"Bridget, you and Mary were friends until Louise moved in. Is that correct?"

"That's so."

"May I ask why your friendship ended so abruptly?"

"It wasn't all of sudden. Mary wanted an unnatural friendship with me I told her I wasn't interested. After that we stayed away from each other as much as possible."

"An unnatural friendship?"

"Like that of Maude and Rose." Louise explained.

"Like that of a man and a woman, Mr. Bowling." Bridget giggled.

Charles' face blazed crimson. "I see."

"Do either of you know if Mary had any other friends or relatives in the area?"

"She had a man once what worked over at the

Kentuck Mine." Louise said. "Talked about how they was going away to San Francisco until he was killed."

"Was his name Joseph?"

"I don't remember if she ever said."

"Mary had that sister down in Carson City." Bridget added. "From the way she talked, her sister was a rich high society lady who had long ago disowned her…."

"Do either of you recall if anyone left the house the night Mary was murdered?"

The women looked at the kitchen door nervously. Charles walked to the doorway and looked down the hall. "We're all alone. There's nothing to be afraid of, no one's listening." He assured them.

"You mean anyone other than the gentlemen callers?" Louise asked.

"Did anyone who lived or worked here leave that night?" He asked.

"Rose and Wing Li did." Bridget said.

"They left together?"

"Didn't I just say so, Mr. Bowling?"

"What time was that?" He asked.

"It must have been sometime after midnight. All the gentlemen were gone. I was hungry so came down to get myself a biscuit before we got busy again. Just as I started to step through to the kitchen I heard the back door open. It was Rose and Wing Li. They were arguing over something. I heard her say, 'That ought to hold her.' And he said, 'Yes, but it wasn't necessary.' I decided it was no business of mine so I just sneaked away before they saw me."

Charles thanked her and looked closely at her face. Such a face didn't need so much powder, especially during daylight hours. "Has someone struck you recently, Bridget?"

Her face turned scarlet. She lowered her head and clenched her fists. "It was…just a…just a misunderstanding with my man."

"Who is he?" Charles demanded. The general believe was that a fallen woman deserved what she got. He saw it differently.

Louise giggled nervously at his naiveté. No girl in their profession would ever mention the names of clients or beaus. To do so would surely mean expulsion from this, or any other, house.

"No matter. After this," she pointed at her left eye. "He's not my man."

Satisfied, Charles said. "That's a good thing. Why did Rose dislike Mary?"

"I don't know." Bridget finally said. "Do you, Louise?"

Louise smiled sadly. "That Rose can be a mean one. She really doesn't care for any of us."

"Ask Wing Li. He'll tell you. Nothing goes on around here that he doesn't know about." Bridget said.

"How do you feel about Wing Li?" Charles asked Louise.

She lowered her voice. "He's mean as Rose." She said eyeing the door nervously.

"Thank you for your time ladies. If you should think of anything else please get in touch with me."

Eighteen

Charles went up to the Barbary Coast more often than any other area of the city. Like its San Francisco namesake, this area near the Divide was the most dangerous place on the Comstock. A string of shanties, boardinghouses and saloons lining South C Street, the coast was home to the city's worst criminal element.

The women who plied their trade in the Barbary Coast's redlight district were without hope. Tossed out of all the finer brothels like the Silver Window, they came here when there was nowhere else to go. Most of them were old, and sick and dying. Mary Hanlon might well have ended up here, he thought as he hitched his horse to the post.

The air in the saloon was heavy with smoke. He chose a seat near the front door. His eyes watered and adjusted to the room's darkness. A boisterous group of miners carried on a loud conversation at the far end of the bar. An old man absently strummed his banjo in the corner.

A plump redheaded bartender smiled at him. "What's your pleasure tonight?" She asked, leaning across the bar seductively.

"Information...I'm looking for Sally Swan."

She laughed loudly. "Why would a good looking gent such as yerself bother with the likes of Sally?

That dried up old harpy's as crazy as they come."

"As special assistant to Police Chief Dolan, I have several questions to ask her concerning a recent murder."

The bartender's demeanor changed. She wiped the bar with a damp towel and scowled at him. "In that case mister, Sally's busy."

"Then I'll wait." He said looking around at the other men. Surely she was smart enough to realize that his presence would quickly take the edge off her customer's enjoyment. There were too many other saloons in town, other saloons that didn't have a policeman sitting at the bar and watching their every movement.

"Sally!" She bellowed. "There's a gent wanting to see you!" She wiped the bar and glared at him. "Hurry now! He's not got all day."

Charles expected anything, but the woman who stumbled out from the backroom. Tall and gaunt with skin as gray as death, she couldn't have been much older than thirty but her stringy limp hair was snow white. She squinted at Charles. "You the one wants me?" She asked perching on the stool next to his.

"Yes Miss Swan. I'm Charles Bowling special assistant to Police Chief Dolan."

She tossed her head back and roared with laughter. "So you're old Dolan's minion are you?"

The description was an accurate one. He let it slide with a smile and a nod.

"While investigating the murder of Mary Hanlon

your name has come to my attention."

"So the lyin doxie finally got herself killed did she? Well good riddance to her. Now why don't you buy me a whiskey and let's drink a toast to the one that did her in."

He tossed two quarters on the bar and the bartender greedily swept them up in her hand.

"What'll it be mister?"

"A glass of water for me please. And get the lady whatever she wants."

Both women cackled loudly at his use of the word 'lady'. "Shoot mister. Sally's no more a lady than you are." The bartender teased.

He ignored the comment. "Now Miss Swan, I don't want you toasting the death of Mary Hanlon. But I don't want you thirsty either."

She smiled and downed her whiskey. "A no good thief, that Mary was, she'd steal anything that wasn't nailed down."

"I understood she used your laudanum on occasion?"

"Used? That what you're calling it now? I'll remember that next time one of you comes here fixing to arrest me for stealing."

"You were asked to leave the Silver Window because of an argument with Mary?"

"Yeah, I finally got tired of her stealing my laudanum and kicked up too big a fuss to suit them. Maude doesn't like screaming and fighting. But it was always Mary who started the fights. And everybody knew it, except Maude. So I was out and Mary stayed."

She pounded her hand on the bar and demanded, "Another whiskey!" It was a privilege rarely allotted her. As long as her newfound benefactor was paying, she was drinking.

The bartender waddled to the bottle and poured Sally another drink. And slapping the glass down she warned, "Better take it easy Sal."

Sally stared at the drink wistfully. "Who you figure killed her?"

"I was hoping you could help me with that." Charles said. "Can you think of anyone who might have wanted to see Mary dead?"

She laughed. "That's easy. Anyone that ever knew her might want to kill her. She stole and she gossiped and she lied. I got shown the door on account of her. Time was, I was a mind to cut her throat myself."

"What changed your mind?"

She gulped her drink. "Why you did. You just told me she was dead." She smiled.

"Do you remember Mary's dial and her spirit communication?" He asked the question feeling silly.

"Her and that Bridget were both a couple of liars…and thieves. Those two would kill their own mothers for the price of a new frock. They were trying to frighten all of us with that hobgoblin stuff. I don't think they believed none of it. It was just a way to find people's secrets."

"What about someone's death being predicted?"

"I don't recall that."

Charles placed a dollar on the bar. "For later." He told the bartender who scooped the bill up as fast as she had the quarters. Charles had seen sick men and women before. Judging by the pallor of her skin, Sally Swan's future was a relatively short one.

Sally smiled brightly. "Thank you kindly, mister."

"One more thing, have you ever heard anything about an unnatural friendship between Rose and Maude?"

Sally chuckled. "Shoot no. Wouldn't believe it if I did." She eyed him suspiciously. "Who told you that malarkey?"

"You are certain there was never any talk about--"

"Bridget got mad at Rose one day and yelled something at her like 'just 'cause you love Maude you don't want none of us being her friend too' something like that."

"What did Rose do?"

"She laughed at her. Told her she was a no good little trollop who'd better mind her manners or she'd be looking for some other place to work. That shut her right up."

"You're certain you don't know anything about Mary Hanlon's murder?"

"I left there and forgot all of them. But you can mark my word it was one of them at the Silver Window. Mayhap Rose got mad and shot her. Could be Bridget and her had a falling out and she stabbed her with that dagger of hers. Could be Wing Li poisoned her. I don't know." She laughed wildly. "Mayhap one of those hobgoblins she talked with did her in."

Nineteen

Chief Dolan's office was the police station on C. Street. In the late afternoon, sunlight streamed into the room through the two large plate glass windows on either side of the door. Dolan's battered mahogany desk was placed directly in front of one window. This enabled him to watch passersby throughout the day. Charles' much smaller cubbyhole desk was behind the chief's so that he too might catch a glimpse of activity on the street.

When the weather turned cold an icy draft seeped through the sill and rimmed the window with a thick coating of frost. On these mornings it was understood that Charles would be the first to arrive. He lit a fire in the stove, and put the coffee on. While the liquid gurgled in the cast iron coffeepot he propped his feet up on his desk and read his previous day's notes.

The fire was usually glowing bright red, the room filled with the rich aroma of coffee, by the time Chief Dolan came through the door complaining about his rheumatism.

On this morning he hung his coat on the peg and quickly sought the warmth of his padded rocker at the stove. Charles pulled up an old ladder back chair and joined him. The two men genuinely liked each other and companionable silence easily fell between them. Finally Dolan turned to Charles and asked.

"Wellsir, what we got facing us this morning?"

This was Charles signal to make his official report of any and everything he had seen or heard during the previous day. While the chief poured steaming coffee from his cup to his saucer and sipped noisily Charles told him what he had learned from Bridget and Louise. Dolan placed his saucer on the stand, and laughed uproariously.

"You mean to tell me you never heard them stories about Maude and Rose?" He asked. "I thought everybody on the Comstock knew that story."

Charles suddenly felt naïve and foolish. "Sally Swan has never heard it."

"Sally Swan! It's a wonder that woman's still on this side of the grave. Her mind's been rotting away for years."

"Do you believe Rose might have tossed Mary out over jealousy?" Charles asked.

"For one thing, that Bridget is a wicked little liar. I wouldn't put too much stock in anything she told me, if I was you, Charlie. Pretty as they come, but the girl would lie when the truth would serve. No boy. Rose ain't jealous of no one, least of all some alcohol sodden strumpet like Mary Hanlon. You're looking for someone with an axe to grind there. Leave it be for a bit boy. We'll find the person who killed her all in good time. "

"Did you know Mary Hanlon?" Charles asked.

"I know all the ladies up at Maude's and those at the Bow Windows, and the Brick as well. But to tell you the truth, I never cared for Mary Hanlon much nohow. She was the sort that didn't belong there. Not that she was too good, mind you. She was just mean and spiteful. A real troublemaker. Whoever it was that killed her was probably someone she done wrong."

Charles didn't like his coffee as strong as the Chief did. He sipped the bitter black liquid slowly. The fire crackled, heating the room until it was stifling, even for the chief. He strode to door and flung it open. Pulling out his watch fob, he studied it intently. "We'll catch him soon enough. But there's still plenty for you to do till then."

That plenty involved running various errands that took up the better part of the morning. When he'd finished, Charles stopped at the dry goods store to ask about a dial. The clerk was a young woman who quickly informed him she didn't hold with people talking with dead people. Further, she added, "I wouldn't tell you where to get one of those things even if I knew. Anyone who plays with that is doing the devil's work."

Smiling to himself, Charles stepped onto the sidewalk just as Wing Li came strolling down C. Street. When he realized that Charles was staring at him, he turned and walked away.

"Wait a minute!" Charles called to the fleeing man. "Wing Li wait!"
Wing Li swiftly covered the uneven wooden sidewalks until Charles finally grabbed him by the sleeve of his black satin jacket in front of Cole's

Emporium.

"I beg your pardon Mr. Bowling." Wing Li said haughtily. "I didn't realize that it was a crime to walk down C. Street."

Charles let go of Wing Li's sleeve. "Why did you turn and run when you saw me?"

"I am in a hurry. Rose's catarrh is causing her much distress. She needs her laudanum right away."

Ignoring the health problems of Rose, Charles asked. "I'm told you know everything that goes on at the Silver Window. Is that true?"

Wing Li's expression changed, Charles had hit a nerve. "Whoever told you that is a liar. I pay no attention to that which doesn't concern me."

"That's odd. You work there don't you?"

"Yes I do." He shrugged. "Yet I am a man who minds his own business. What goes on there is none of mine so I pay no attention." Wing Li stepped toward the emporium's door.

"I really must get that laudanum back to Rose."

"No one is stopping you from doing so." And as Wing Li turned to walk away, Charles said. "I'd better not find that you have lied to me."

Wing Li smirked and silently walked away.

.

Twenty

For the first time since the discovery of Mary Hanlon's body, Charles allowed himself to relax. Comfortably perched on the settee, he listened as the wind whistled through the trees, tossing low branches across the windows. Gazing at the roaring fire that burned in the grate, he looked across the room at the others and thought not for the first time, how truly blessed he was.

Her knitting needles click clacking rhythmically, Sarah said "I can't stop wondering whether or not the killer believed Mary Hanlon could actually speak to the dead. If so…She may have stumbled onto a secret he didn't want discovered."

Benjamin agreed. "It's as good as any theory."

"Who believes that stuff is possible?" Charles asked.

Therese smiled at him. "Some people believe in it very strongly. Maybe you would too if you had attended Mrs. Lloyd's lecture." She teased.

"Did Mary Hanlon know something the killer didn't want anyone else to find out about?"

"Perhaps it came to her through the dial." Agnes suggested.

"Or she inadvertently said something that made the killer think so." Benjamin said.

"I've made a list of suspects if you'd care to hear about them." Charles said.

Lottie stared at him intently. "Yes by all means dear."

"Well," he began, "there is the sister, Mrs. Bramwell. Who would not want to have her good name sullied. And there's the husband Joseph

Hanlon, that all presumed to be dead. Sally Swan's at death's door but she may have had help in killing Mary Hanlon."

Sarah sniffed. "Well I would think that either one of those two—"

"And why not Mrs. Bramwell?" Therese asked.

Before Sarah could explain, Charles held up his hand. "You've not let me finished. There's Maude and her people at the brothel. Any one of them may have had reason to kill Mary Hanlon."

"But didn't you say that you thought there may have been two killers?" Agnes asked.

"The Coombs said they heard someone say 'you've made a murderer of me twice.' Leastwise Mr. Coombs heard that. Mrs. Coombs heard someone speaking Chinese." Charles explained.

"Humph! Jane Coombs wouldn't know Chinese from a barn owl." Sarah said.

"Surely she would know if someone was speaking it…even if she didn't understand what was being said." Agnes said, inspecting the seam she'd just sewn. "I can't understand why anyone would give away such a fine garment."

"Isn't that one of Miriam's cast offs?" Lottie asked.

Agnes held the bottle green velvet dress up for all to see. "She is so thrifty and this is a very fashionable shade."

Sarah touched dress. "Yes it does seem rather new and fashionable for the parsimonious Miriam to donate…She usually waits until a garment is well out of style."

While fashion was being discussed Charles thought now might be a good time to show them the earring..

"I found this at the murder scene."

They crept closer and gazed at the earring. "This is an expensive piece of jewelry." Sarah said taking the earring. "The work is very intricate."

Benjamin asked. "Did it belong to the dead woman."

Sarah laughed mockingly. "Honestly! Do you think such a woman would own fine jewelry? And why would he steal only one earring." She gasped. "Or perhaps the murderer is a woman and she dropped this at the scene."

Charles said. "But she would have to be an exceptionally strong woman."

Agnes crept closer. Reaching for the earring, she said. "Let me see that…Oh my. No, this can't be! I don't understand. "

"What don't you understand?" Charles asked.

"That is Miriam's earring!"

"Miriam is the killer?" Benjamin asked incredulous.

"Of course not!" She gasped. "But this is her earring!"

"Are you certain?"

"I am. I remember when Dan bought them for her…He had been away on a business trip. Upon his return he gave them to her… Why not ask Dan? He will tell you."

"I'll do that." Charles said placing the earring back in his pocket.

Twenty One

The Eldons/Waters home was located in an area known as "Millionaires' Row" because of the men who'd struck it rich in the silver mines and chosen to erect their mansions here on B. Street high above the rest of the city.

A steep rock staircase led from the street to the front porch. At the top of the stairs was a tall ornamental iron fence. Behind its gate stood the elegant home with its three-story tower, mansard roof and dormer windows. During the spring and summer months the yard surrounding the house was filled with bushes and flowers of every color. Now there were only the bare gray stalks and stems. Regardless of the season, the Eldons/Waters home bespoke its owner's wealth and prestige.

Charles climbed the stairs hoping to find Dan in better control of himself than he was at the cemetery. He rang the ornate doorbell and gazed out across the Comstock.

A bleary eyed Dan opened the door. Crying again, Charles thought.

"Charles, please. Please come in." He stepped aside and led Charles down the marble hallway to a large room at the rear of the house. Heavy maroon drapes hung at the window and blotted out the daylight. The room reeked of stale cigars. As Charles eyes adjusted to the darkness he noticed books, magazines and maps scattered everywhere. Dan pulled the drapes open. "I apologize. I do my best thinking after dark." He explained.

Sunlight flooded the room. Its furnishings were coated with a thick layer of dust. Two brown leather chairs were placed at a large roll top desk. Each was piled with newspapers. No woman in the world would allow such an atrocity. This room must surely be off limits to the housekeeper.

"Have a seat." Dan motioned to one of the chairs and plopped in the other. "Can I get you anything to drink, a glass of water...perhaps a whiskey?"

"Nothing thanks. How are you holding up Dan?"

Dan fell back into his chair. "Not good. Not good at all. The only bright spot is that my darling Miriam is returning." A smile crossed his face and was gone. "I'm afraid she won't be happy with what I've discovered though. Theodore was a good man, but he left us heavily in debt. I had no idea he had commenced loaning his own money to men who hadn't the means or the intentions of ever repaying him."

It doesn't help that Miriam is a spendthrift. Charles thought.

"By the time all his debts are settled there'll be nothing left. I am hoping that we won't have to sell the house. This will be a terrible shock to Miriam." He smiled again. "She loves to flit about and spend money on the silliest of trinkets."

Dan pointed the other side of the room. "See that silly globe in the corner, and that horrid drinking horn on the wall there? Miriam's ideas of manly décor, and when my wife gets an idea in her head, there's no dislodging it. No, she isn't going to like this financial turn of events at all. But you didn't come here to listen to my woes."

Embarrassed for the other man, Charles stammered, "I'm sorry to hear that, Dan." He held up the earring. "Agnes thinks this belongs to Miriam. Do you recognize it?"

"Well, it certainly looks like one of Miriam's. May I?" Dan asked reaching for the earring. Holding it close to his eyes he demanded, "Where did you get this?"

"Near the body of the woman who was killed out in the canyon."

"That trollop that got herself murdered?"

Charles nodded silently.

"That's impossible. I had this set designed for Miriam two years ago. But...I am certain hers are in her jewelry box. She never takes any of her jewelry to Europe."

"That's odd. Most women want to show off her baubles."

"She does," Dan laughed, "but in this instance she's afraid one of her relatives might think she is wealthy and ask her for things."

"Doesn't it take a certain amount of wealth to travel as often as Miriam does?"

"Well yes." Dan smiled. "But what man can understand the workings of the female mind for goodness sakes?"

Dan passed the earring back to him. "I have no

explanation for this."

"Will you see if Miriam's earrings are still in her jewelry box?"

While Dan went about the task, Charles read the plaque beneath the hideous drinking horn. *For my loving husband Daniel Bryce Waters.*

At the window, he watched as the housekeeper daubed a soapy rag at a large braided rug that hung on the clothesline. As she dipped the rag in a pail water a big yellow tabby cat brushed happily against her ankles. She wrung the rag and slung it over the clothesline. Her chores forgotten for the time being, the housekeeper dried her hands on her checkered apron. She bent and stroked the cat, then gently picked up the fat yellow ball of fur and cuddled it close to her. Watching her thus occupied, Charles sneezed. He loved cats too, but couldn't live with one. To be near a cat for long meant runny eyes and sneezing.

Dan returned to the room and stared out the window. "Humph! Her and that cat! It's a wonder she gets any work done, the time she spends playing with that creature….Just as long as it stays outdoors, I suppose."

Charles smiled to himself. Apparently Dan was not a cat fancier.

Dan rapped loudly on the window. Without a backward glance, the housekeeper put the cat down and went back to work on the rug. "She is so lazy sometimes." He explained.

"Is she deaf?" Charles asked.

"No she's not. But why do you ask?"

"She didn't acknowledge your tapping on the window."

"Who knows why any female does what she does?" Dan chuckled.

"Did you find Miriam's earrings?"

Dan handed him two earrings, identical in every way to the one he held in his hands.

"I had these earrings specially designed for Miriam. And they were not cheap, believe me. And yet you're telling me this murdered woman somehow managed to have a duplicate?

"Apparently so."

Dan's face turned scarlet. He gasped for air. Placing Miriam's earrings on the desk, he plopped down in his chair. "That is absurd! How could this, this sort of woman, have a pair of earrings like Miriam's?"

"Perhaps Miriam had another pair made." Charles said.

"Why on earth would she do such a thing?" Dan asked springing to his feet.

"She might have lost one, or been afraid she would lose one" Charles answered.

"Even if that were true, and I doubt it…How could Miriam's earrings end up with a dead whore?"

How indeed, Charles wondered. "I'm not sure how it all fits together just yet Dan. Who did you buy the earrings from? Maybe he can explain it."

"I had a jeweler in California—Monterey, but the name slips my mind." Dan glanced around the room. "I'm sure I have the receipt here somewhere…I'll see if I can find it for you."

Charles surveyed the cluttered room. He doubted anyone could find anything in this room.

"If you should come across it," he said, still wondering why the housekeeper hadn't turned around.

Twenty Two

Feeling out of place in his evening attire, Benjamin, sat between Agnes and Lottie, and at the other end of the long table, Charles was between Therese and Sarah. Opposite them, Dan Waters sat beside a silver haired widow. Inviting Dan in his wife's stead was a touch of brilliance on Agnes' part, and watching him and the widow, she silently congratulated herself on that brilliance. With him in attendance, no one would dare whisper that Miriam was cavorting in Europe with her English nobleman. All talk of untoward activity would be silenced.

As was the case each year, no expense had been spared on the charitable society's event. The table was lined with candelabras. A crystal chandelier hung high overhead and twinkling every color of the rainbow and providing light for the celebrants to dine by. Gas lamp sconces burned brightly on every wall.

Across the table Dan and the widow engaged in animated conversation. For the first time since his father in law's death, Dan was laughing out loud. Charles smiled knowing the real reason for Dan's joviality was Miriam's imminent return and not the widow's brilliant repartee. He turned to Therese and said, "You look especially lovely tonight, Therese.

She blushed just as Martin Harris walked up. "Good evening ladies, you all look quite charming this evening." And as an afterthought, he turned to Charles and asked. "Charles, might I have a word?"

They walked to an out of the way corner of the room and Martin demanded, "Are you and Dolan making any headway in this case?"

"These things take time."

"I take it you've no suspects."

"We have a few suspects and we're working on the assumption that two people may have been-"

"Two! It took two people to kill an old whore out in the canyon?

"That's not what I said."

Martin leaned close to Charles. "You and Dolan better have this killer sitting in jail before the month is out." He stood back and patted Charles on the back. "You don't want to disappoint me on this. That would not be wise for either one of your jobs."

With those words he strode away, leaving Charles unclenching his fists.

Twenty Three

With Charles and Therese out at Six Mile Canyon for the day, Lottie, Agnes and Sarah hired a buggy at the B. Street livery. After telling Benjamin they were headed up to Gold Hill for the quilting bee, Agnes drove the buggy down to Chinatown.

"You found her here?" Therese asked as Charles drove the buggy up to the large boulder and jumped to the ground. The snow was melted. It was a warmer than usual fall day, the sky a deep autumn blue and sunlight glinting on the rocks. Therese tried to imagine how it must have been on the night Mary Hanlon was killed.

"Poor thing was probably shivering out here in the darkest coldest part of the night." She said as Charles helped her down from the buggy. "What a pitiful way to die. Oh Charles, promise me that he won't get away with it. We, that is you, will catch him won't you?" She asked.

Charles smiled at her. "I will."

"I hope so." She said. "It would be terrible to think that he was free to kill others."

"That won't happen." Charles said.

"Why on earth was she out here? Do you think she came out here to meet someone?"

"I think the answer to all this is at the Silver Window."

Therese gasped. "That would mean that a woman

could be the killer."

"It's possible."

"But not probable." She answered.

"Mr. and Mrs. Coombs both agree that there were two people coming out of the canyon that night."

"A man and a woman?"

"The Coombs seem to think it was two men"

"So your suspects are women, except for Joseph Hanlon of course."

"You've forgotten Wing Li." Charles said. "He and Rose could easily kill someone."

Benjamin gently closed the new leather bound book, lit a cigar and puffed on it happily.

The ladies were in Gold Hill doing what they did best, wielding their needles and wagging their tongues. Charles and Therese were together somewhere and he was alone in the parlor. He welcomed his solitude. It gave him time to think about what needed doing in the case.

He was certain that he and he alone, knew best how to solve this case and catch the killer. Charles was clever. But he was young. And being young, he often missed the finer points.

In going over the facts of this case, he thought of something the others had overlooked. While they were all away, he would take the opportunity to look into it further. And so, with the late autumn afternoon sun glowing all around him, Benjamin strode purposely down the hill toward C. Street.

Twenty Four

They'd been here long enough to see the crescent moon rise over Sugar Loaf. As it darkened, the sky filled with stars and a chill hung in the air.

Pulling her shawl tight around her, Therese asked. "Did the Coombs see Mary Hanlon walking to the canyon?"

""I didn't ask them."

"Maybe we should stop at their place on the way home." She said.

In answer to Charles' knock, Pedro rushed to the door loudly barking

"Hush boy!" Mort commanded, opening the door.

"Why Charlie back so soon? And you got a young lady with you." He stepped aside. "C'mon in then."

Seated in front of the fire, Mrs. Coombs stood and smiled.

"Here have a seat." She said.

"No thank you Mam." Charles said. "This is my friend Therese Gunderson, Mr. and Mrs. Coombs."

Therese smiled warmly at them.

"Pleased I'm sure." Mrs. Coombs said.

"I've a question for you, Mort. It may, or may not, be important."

Mort plopped on the pallet. "What is it, Charlie?"

"You told me that you saw a buggy with two people coming out of the canyon the night of the murder. Now I want you to think about this carefully. Did you see anyone walking toward the canyon that day?"

Mort scratched his head as if to contemplate his answer. "Yes! I was skinning rabbits. The ladies pay right nice for the fur." He explained, smiling at Therese. "I heard someone crying. First I thought it was the warning whistle from the Belcher Mine, it's almost like a scream. I looked and seen this woman walking down the canyon trail. She weren't walking so much as she was hobbling. It set me to wondering why a woman would be heading out there alone so close to nightfall. "Course I can think of one reason." He smiled slyly at his wife.

"Mortimer Coombs, you old reprobate!" She snapped. "There's a young lady present!"

"Apologies miss." He said to Therese who smiled at him.

"She stopped a spell. Then she walked on. She was crying and wiping her nose. T'was no concern of mine, so I went back to my work."

"Do you recall what she looked like?" Charles asked.

"Well she wasn't all that close, but I could tell she weren't no girl. She had golden colored hair is alls I know."

"Was she alone?"

"Yessiree Bob!"

"No one was following her?" Therese asked.

"No Mam! Not a solitary soul."

It was well after midnight when they left the

Coombs' place and headed back up the hill to the C. Street Livery. There they dropped the buggy off and walked the short distance to the rooming house.

"Perhaps Mary Hanlon hoped to meet someone. But who would go out there after dark?" Therese asked.

"Someone that didn't want to be seen."

"Mrs. Bramwell!" Therese said. "She has a reputation to uphold. She could have gone out there and killed her own sister to keep from sullying it."

"That's farfetched." Charles said.

"Is it?" Therese asked.

Twenty Five

Lottie woke first and crept into the dining room. She and Agnes were finishing their second cup of coffee when Benjamin sat down at the table. Sarah appeared next with a towel wrapped around her jaw. The tooth she'd ignored for so long was finally exacting its revenge.

Therese wandered in half asleep, followed by Charles who yawned widely as he pulled his chair out. No one spoke. They sipped their coffee and picked at the muffin tray.

After a nod from Agnes, Lottie said to Charles who absently buttered a muffin. "I, that is we, have something to confess, dear."

Sarah moaned her disapproval at what she knew

was coming. Agnes stirred her coffee absently.

"We didn't go to Gold Hill for a quilting bee." Lottie blurted.

"Don't tell me you went up to the Silver Window to see Maude Banning." Charles smiled.

Lottie gasped.

"Surely even you three wouldn't be so bold as to attempt to gather clues at a house of ill repute." Benjamin said, chuckling at the thought.

"Naafunee." Sarah snapped, not about to let a toothache prevent her from offering an opinion.

"No it isn't" Lottie agreed.

"We went to the Wo Sing Café." Agnes announced, smirking at Benjamin. "We hired a buggy and drove down--"

"Foolish women!" Charles snapped. "That is nothing but a cover for an opium den. You could all have been robbed, or murdered."

"How were we to know that?" Agnes asked.

"One more reason you shouldn't go wandering around where you know you ought not be. Wo Sing has one of the largest dens in town down in their basement." Charles said. "It's certainly not an area for ladies day or night."

"Women should be able to go wherever they please, whenever they please." Therese said.

"Women have no business in certain places!" Benjamin said. "Regardless of what they please…What if you had ran into trouble?"

"I'd have shot dead anyone who meant to harm us." Agnes said grabbing for a piece of bacon.

Therese smiled approvingly. They hadn't gone to

the area without the protection of a loaded pistol.

"We only wanted to be a part of the investigation." Lottie explained.

"And did you discover anything?" Charles asked.

"No nothing." Lottie said gazing at her lap. "But then there was one peculiar incident. Benjamin, do you remember the stout woman at Piper's the other night?" She asked.

He nodded and she continued. "Well we saw her run out of the building and this Chinese man went after her and they appeared to be arguing over something."

"Perhaps I ought to pay the place a visit myself." Charles said absently.

"If I remember correctly Martin Harris talked of cleaning up these opium dens in his campaign speeches, when do you suppose he'll start?" Benjamin asked.

"Chief Dolan says we can look for some changes starting after the first of the year."

"Not soon enough for me." Benjamin sniffed.

Twenty Six

Windswept clouds pushed eastward splitting open and releasing torrents of rain. Lightning sliced across the night sky. Thunder rumbled and roared in the distance.

The parlor was warmed by the roaring fire. While the women did their sewing, the men read.

Benjamin, his spectacles pushed low on the bridge of his nose, was so absorbed in *War and Peace*, that he was oblivious to the women's conversation. Charles was equally absorbed in the newspaper.

A loud crack of thunder roared high overhead. Lightning crackled, and in that instant the sky was a bright as daylight.

"Oh my." Lottie gasped fearfully. "That lightning sounds close. I hope it doesn't strike the city."

Charles put the paper down. "Don't worry, Aunt Lottie. That was miles away. Probably down in Dayton or Carson City."

Benjamin looked up from *War and Peace* which was getting very interesting. Pierre Bezukhov had joined the freemasons and was seeing the world through different eyes.

"And if the lightning should strike us, you have nothing to fear. Two of Engine Company One's finest firemen are right here in your parlor." He boasted; then back to Pierre and his transition, he went.

Sarah sneered at Benjamin. She doubted the statement's veracity as far as he was concerned.

Therese heard the thumping first. "What's that?" She asked. "Shhh. Listen!"

As they did so, the thumping grew louder and more persistent. Someone was fiercely pounding on the front door.

Charles opened the door to find Chief Dolan.

"Chief," Charles said, stepping aside to let the older man enter.

Dolan wiped his muddy boots on the braided rug inside the doorway. "Sorry to disturb you at home Charlie. But we got ourselves some big problems tonight and I need your help."

Curious, Benjamin and the women crept into the hallway and stared at the chief who dripped water on the freshly polished wood floor.

"Evenin' Ladies, Ben." He said, doffing his hat. "As I was saying--"

"Won't you please come into the parlor Chief Dolan?" Lottie asked.

"No thank you Mrs. Duckworth, mam. I'm sopping wet and not wanting to ruin your furniture." He turned to Charles and whispered. "Can we talk somewhere else Charlie?"

"Come around back to the kitchen porch."

. Dolan nodded. "Yes. I'll go to the back." Then pointedly, "Ladies good evening."

As the front door closed behind him Sarah said. "I suppose that means this conversation is for men's ears only."

Therese rolled her eyes. "Some men and their ridiculously antiquated ideas of decorum."

"He is merely trying to shield you ladies from some unpleasantness." Benjamin assured her.

"We're strong." Therese called to the retreating Benjamin who followed Charles to the back porch.

"A Godforsaken night if I ever seen one." The chief said wiping his boots.

"Where's the ladies?" He asked.

"In the parlor, fuming about being left out." Benjamin smiled.

Charles dragged three chairs out to the porch from Mrs. Noonan's tidy kitchen and shoved one toward the Chief.

Dolan sat and rubbed his painful knees. "I was hoping the nightshift could handle all this. But we just got too damn much going on."

"Can I get you something to drink Chief?" Charles asked.

Dolan smiled at him. "Wouldn't happen to have any tarantula juice would you?"

"I believe so," Charles said dashing back into the kitchen.

He selected one of the largest tumblers and filled it to the rim with the amber liquid. Knowing Dolan's proclivity for nighttime whiskey, he took the bottle with him when he returned to the porch.

Dolan downed the whiskey in one gulp. "Thanks. That hit the spot, Charlie."

"Care for another?" Charles offered, knowing full well Dolan could drink the whole bottle and still be thirsty for more.

The chief drank his second drink as quickly as the first. "Wellsir, we got us a villainous night all right. This wind is tearin' up the whole town! Blew the roof clean off the McIntyre Stable. People get all stirred up in this kinda weather. Some miner up on the Divide got in a fight with his wife…slit her throat…and then the poor bastard took the butcher knife out to the privy and did hisself in. That had to hurt like hell."

He looked toward the kitchen to make certain no one was eavesdropping. "I trust the ladies are out of earshot?"

Charles nodded and the Chief continued. "Course that's not the reason I came by. It's your friend Dan Waters."

"Has something happened to him?" Charles asked.

"We got him locked up at the jail drunk as a skunk."

Charles stared at him in disbelief. "Dan doesn't drink."

Dolan lowered his voice to a whisper. "Poor bastard got hisself a letter that says his wife's been killed in some boat accident in Switzerland somewhere."

"Man alive!" Charles gasped. "How much more can he take?"

"S'actly my thoughts. That's why we arrested him. He was down at Jack Murphys trying to pick a fight with some miner. Could have got hisself beat half to death, or killed."

"Damn fool!" Benjamin said.

"Thank you Chief. Dan will need every friend he has right now. I'll come up and get him. " Charles said.

"Who will tell Agnes?" Benjamin asked. "She will be heartbroken."

Dolan and Charles looked at him. Finally Dolan spoke. "I was you, Ben I'd break it to the ladies gently." And laying a gnarled hand on Charles' shoulder he added. "And Charlie, if you're thinking of bringing old Dan back here with you, you'd best fill him with a coupla pots of strong coffee first. He's been using some right salty language." He eyed the bottle of whiskey longingly. "Maybe I'll have one more swallow afore I head out." He said holding his empty glass toward Charles.

After telling the women only that it was a matter of grave importance, Charles and Benjamin threw on their overcoats and walked out into the rainstorm. They walked the short distance to the jail in silence, pushing against the wind.

They found Dan sobbing incoherently in a small cell at the back of the jail. "Dan old man, it's me Charles. Benjamin and I have come to pour hot coffee down you and sober you up." He said feigning cheerfulness.

Dan leapt at the bars like a wild man. "Oh Charles. Thank God you've come. She's dead! Dead! Do you hear me?"

Charles nodded silently. There was nothing he could say. Except get his friend reasonably sober and take him home to sleep it off. The jailer produced a pot of coffee as dark and strong as Charles' morning brew.

"There could be a mistake." Dan cried, drinking one cup after another.

"I'm sure they have a good idea it is her, Dan."

"But why did this happen to my Miriam?" Dan demanded slamming his empty cup on the table. "How can I live without her? Oh God! This just isn't fair!"

Charles looked at Benjamin who shrugged his shoulders and said. "Life is seldom fair, Dan. As men, we must deal with what's handed us."

Dan took no comfort in the older man's words. He sobbed hysterically. "But why did my wife have to die? Why couldn't it have been some other man's?"

"That's a question none of us can ever answer." Charles said calmly.

Half the night was gone before Charles and Benjamin stood on either side of Dan and steadied him up the street to a spare room at the rooming house. There, he tossed and turned the remainder of the night away, while Charles and Benjamin broke the news to the women.

Agnes sunk to her knees crying "No, no I don't believe you."

Lottie, Sarah and Therese hovered over her.

"She may need a glass of sherry to calm herself." Benjamin said.

"I'll get it." Therese said, scampering toward the kitchen.

Agnes allowed Charles to help her to her feet and to lead her to the large sofa in the parlor. Therese returned bearing the glass of Sherry. "Drink it, dear. It will help." Lottie said.

Agnes took the glass and downed it in one drink. "Would you like another?" Therese asked.

"No I would not. " Turning to Charles, Agnes said. "I don't know what happened, but I know one thing-- this is not the truth. Miriam did not die in a boat accident. "

"She's gone." Lottie said taking her friends hand. "You must accept that, Agnes."

"No! Charles you've got to look into this. Someone is lying. Those people in Europe probably poisoned her accidently and—"

"She was on that boat, Agnes. And it sank." Charles said.

"No she was not!"

Denial, Benjamin had seen it more times than he cared to count. "Perhaps a good night sleep will make you feel better." He said.

"Yes, yes." The others agreed. And Agnes was led to her bedroom.

Lottie gave her friend time to prepare for bed and then went to her room and sat on the edge of the bed. She was there to offer comfort, soothing words and a willing ear.

"This is not right, Lottie."

"I know dear, but these things—"

Agnes suddenly sat up. "You don't understand! We've been so involved with the murder of that Hanlon woman, we're not seeing everything."

The two women had been friends since childhood, but Lottie was having trouble following her friend's thoughts. "What on earth does that mean?" She asked, plumping the other woman's pillow.

Leaning against her pillow, Agnes took Lottie's hands in her own. "I'm not sure, but there is something---something we're missing."

"Poor dear. You've had a nasty shock." Lottie soothed.

"No! This isn't about Miriam." Agnes said. "It's that Hanlon woman." Tears rolled down her face. "Miriam disliked little boats—she was terrified of water. She would not--someone is lying."

Lottie stood. "I suggest we get a good night's sleep and look at all this fresh tomorrow."

Agnes slid down into the covers. "Good night, Lottie."

Lottie blew out the lamp. "Sleep well." She whispered knowing that her friend would sleep very little.

Twenty Seven

Virginia City stood cloaked in darkness. The storm had moved off toward the east. In the midst of the worst of it, customers had left early and everyone at the Silver Window was fast asleep. Bridget crept up to the back door, stopped and listened. She was safe. No one was stirring. She turned the doorknob slowly and stepped into the kitchen.

She gasped when she realized that Rose and Wing Li were sitting at the kitchen table.

Long suspicious that some of the girls were running out at night to be with husbands and boyfriends, they'd set a trap. Bridget was the first to be ensnared.

"Where have you been?" Rose asked lighting a lamp. "You know the rules and yet you chose to disobey them. Do you want us to kick you out?"

Bridget eyed Rose coldly. "If you think you're

going to chase me away like you did poor old Mary you'd better have another think."

"Perhaps we should tell Maude about this. She'd certainly waste no time in showing you the door." Wing Li smirked, his eyes glittering with distaste.

Rose smiled. "But there is a way out for you, Bridget. If you tell us who else is involved in this chicanery we'll overlook tonight's incident. Right, Wing Li?"

He smirked at Bridget. "As I see it, you've got no choice but to tell us."

"What are you going to do if I don't? Kill me like you did Mary?" Bridget snarled.

"How dare you accuse me of murder, you little strumpet!" Rose seethed.

Wing Li laughed cruelly. "If we had, do you suppose we would hesitate to also kill you?"

Fear crossed Bridget's face. "I didn't say anything to anyone... Honestly, I didn't tell!"

"Tell what, you silly little strumpet? Now tell us, who else is sneaking out?" Rose demanded.

Bridget plopped onto a chair. "I know you killed Mary and I've got nothing more to say to you."

"Why didn't you tell that pompous Charles Bowling?" Rose taunted.

"How do you know I didn't?" Bridget taunted.

"I listened at the doorway." Rose bragged. "And I heard every word you told him."

Bridget threw back her head and laughed wildly. "You're just a jealous old witch. Jealous 'cause no man looks at you the way they look at me." She patted her thick head of hair. "I'm pretty. And you're not!"

"Your good looks won't last, I can guarantee you that." Rose laughed. "Charles Bowling is not important. Surely you realize that Maude couldn't run this place without us. One word from either of us and you'll be out that door just like your friend Mary was. Tell her Wing Li!"

"Mary wasn't a friend of mine!" Bridget said.

"You're a little liar who'd better not forget that we're running things here." Wing Li said. "Maude needs us."

"No, she does not!" Bridget declared.

"If you can keep your mouth shut we might be able to help one another." He said.

"You and the others enjoy coming and going at will. That can be arranged. You can have all the freedom you want. However, Rose and I want something in return. Now, can you keep your mouth shut?"

Bridget nodded, and Wing Li continued. "Someone is sneaking out and bringing opium back to Maude. We want to know who that person is so that we can throw her out."

"Was Mary--"

"Mary is dead." Rose said. "There's no point in discussing her."

Bridget sighed. "I--I'm pleased that you know it isn't me."

"Mary wasn't supplying Maude with opium. And there is no need to tremble." Wing Li laughed. "No one is going to hurt you."

Twenty Eight

Dan came to the table, haggard and drawn. Agnes, red eyed and sniffling into a lace trimmed handkerchief, sat protectively near him.

Lottie heaped eggs and bacon onto a plate and placed it before him. "It will do you good to eat a hearty breakfast, Dan." She assured the new widower. "Miriam would want you to."

Sarah who'd recently had a tooth pulled, said nothing. Dan Waters was a grown man, if he wanted to eat he would. If he didn't, he wouldn't. He had to eat sooner or later. He was skinny as a rail and couldn't afford to go hungry for very long. But why press the matter this morning? It wouldn't bring his wife back.

Benjamin still slept. But sleep would have to wait for Charles who had a full day's work ahead of him. He hurriedly ate a biscuit and patted Dan on the back. "Sorry to rush, but there's been more problems up on the Divide."

Dan stood and stretched. "Thank you Agnes, Lottie. I don't know what…" He stopped and stared at the wall. "I need to go home and be alone."

"That is the last thing you need, Dan." Lottie said.

She thought of the man on Sutton Street. When his wife died during childbirth he was so distraught, he went down to the cellar and hanged himself. The pain of losing a loved one was difficult to live with. She knew only too well. After the death of her beloved husband she'd cried until there were no tears left.

She was strong, and Dan was not. Maybe it was the difference between men and women and how they dealt with grief. She looked at Dan and wondered if he was capable of taking his own life like the foolish man on Sutton Street had.

Yes, she decided. He was. "Would you like Agnes and me to go with you, Dan? You could pack a few things and come stay with us until you--"

"Yes Dan. That's an excellent suggestion. "Agnes cut in. She too had her doubts concerning his abilities to cope with his situation.

"Leave the man alone." Sarah said. "He knows what he needs to do."

This wasn't consideration for Dan so much as it was her fear that they would next invite him to move into Ducks and Deeks. And God forbid that, she said to herself.

"It's very kind of you ladies. But I need to be alone right now. There are so many things that I must attend to." Tears welled up in his eyes. "Plans for Miriam's…"

"Oh Dan our poor poor Miriam." Agnes cried.

Dan rushed to her. They clung to one another, sobbing in shared sorrow.

Twenty Nine

Grumbling about not getting enough sleep, Chief Dolan arrived at the office later than usual. He'd spent half the night up at the Divide sorting out two killings and a suicide, and he was tired. If he could have he would have stayed home and slept. He poured himself a saucer full of hot coffee and plopped down at his desk. "I reckon Dan's got hisself one miserable headache this morning."

Charles shrugged. "Under the circumstances…"

"Martin and me got a meeting at ten. He wants to know what we're doing in this Mary Hanlon thing, go over how we handle murder from now on." He chuckled. "Wants to see every murdering man swing I guess."

"He takes his job very seriously." Charles said.

"That he does Charlie." Dolan said, absently puffing on his cigar. "Between you and me, I don't like the man. I know some think he may one day be governor. Good God I hope not. He's the kind of man who steps on anybody to get what he wants."

Charles nodded. He shared the chief's dislike of Harris.

"It was sure foolish of Dan to go out on a wild drunk like what he did last night. Was he tryin' to get hisself killed?"

"He'll be okay once he gets over the shock." Charles assured him.

The chief sat up straight. "Think so?"

"He got drunk last night that doesn't mean he's about to kill himself."

"I've seen a lot of things in my time Charlie. If Dan kills hisself it won't surprise me a whit."

Charles frowned. "Dan's stronger than that."

"Mayhap you're right," Dolan said. "Still I reckon his wife's death will be hard for him. He's not the sort to do well on his own, him being henpecked. He needs a woman to tell him what to do."

"There are plenty of women here in Virginia City who'd be willing to take on the job." Charles smiled.

"Once word gets out the scheming females in this town will be after him like a herd of buffalo." Dolan chuckled.

"I need to take a couple hours in the next few days to follow a hunch, Chief." Charles said.

"This something your aunt and the meddling spinsters up at Ducks and Deeks been tellin' you?" Dolan asked, pouring himself another cup of coffee.

"They don't know anything about it."

"Keep it that way. I 'member the last time they tried to play policeman." Dolan laughed. "Ben shoulda knew better, He was—"

'I've told them to stay out of police business, Chief. This idea might not mean anything, but I want to follow through."

"If it'll keep Martin Harris outta our hair I'm all for it, Charlie."

Thirty

"That was a delightful meal. Thank you for inviting me this evening Lottie," Dan said. "I don't know what I would have done without you."

Agnes, who was seated next to him on the velvet sofa, patted his hand gently. "We shall all miss our dear Miriam." She daubed at her eyes with a linen hanky.

"I have ordered a lovely angel headstone. Miriam would have loved…" He fought back tears. "Some may think it foolish of me to go to such expense, but my darling deserves nothing less."

Benjamin studied Dan. Men should never give in to their emotions like this. The ladies were only making matters worse by heaping pity on him.

Benjamin finally spoke. "It is difficult, but you mustn't allow yourself to fall apart."

Dan nodded silently.

"I wish you would consider staying in Virginia City." Lottie said. "It's important to be around friends at a time like this."

"Too many sad memories for me here," Dan explained. "I've decided to make a new start somewhere else. I believe it's what Miriam would have…" Dan shook with emotion as the tears came uncontrollably.

"I am sure she would have wanted you to be happy." Agnes said soothingly.

Benjamin stared at Dan in disgust. Such a display in another man was more than he could bear. Solving this man's problems, horrible as they might be, was not helping them to catch Mary Hanlon's killer.

Charles said. "Give it some time man. You've been through a terrible ordeal with losing Theodore and now Miriam."

Therese agreed. "There's no need to rush into such a decision."

Sarah said. "Of course you may have your own reasons." Her voice trailed off. The last thing she wanted was for him to move into Ducks and Deeks.

Dan nodded.

"Have you caught the murderer yet?" He asked in a weak attempt to change the subject.

"As it turns out, her dead husband is very much alive. And what a scoundrel, he is." Charles said.

"There's a difference between being a scoundrel and a killer." Agnes reminded him.

"But this man is just cold and calculating enough--"

"So is that Wing Li up at the Silver Window" Benjamin said. "Of course he probably doesn't have as strong a motive as Joseph Hanlon does." He thought of a story he'd recently read in his Police Gazette, and said.

"In most cases it's the spouse who does the killing. Woman or man makes no difference."

"I don't believe Joseph Hanlon did it." Therese said. "He's certainly evil enough. But remember, when he wanted to escape Mary he faked his own death. That hardly seems like something a killer would do."

"I think the killer will turn out to be someone at the bawdy house." Lottie said. You're right, Benjamin. Wing Li, or maybe even Maude Banning herself."

"Humph!" Sarah sniffed. "With all that Bramwell money at her disposal Mrs. Bramwell could have paid some rowdy to do her dirty work. She would be my first choice for wanting her sister dead and forgotten. Imagine having a relative like Mary Hanlon."

Charles looked at Sarah thoughtfully. "This could have been a murder for hire."

Feeling left out Dan said. "They say families do some strange things to one another."

"She may have lied to us about not having seen her sister in several years." Charles said. "One of the women at the Silver Window remembers a lady coming to the place in what she described as a 'fine coach.' She told me the woman was covered in a dark veil and that she and Mary got into a screaming match. They had to be pulled away from one another."

"That does sound like her." Therese agreed. "But why on earth—"

"What about Wing Li?" Lottie asked. "Maybe he had a strong motive also."

"I don't think so." Charles said. "Wing Li might well have been the only friend Mary Hanlon had in this world."

Thirty One

At the book store, there was as much gossip as there were books, especially with the news of Dan Waters being a new widower. Every woman with a single relative under the age of fifty secretly planned a bit of match making.

"Do you suppose he will go to the expense of erecting an angel headstone over an empty grave?" The coroner's wife asked.

When her question went unanswered she said, "I don't see him without a wife for long. His kind always needs a woman around to point them in the right direction. Has anyone noticed how young and pretty the Waters' housekeeper is?"

"The way she flounces around, she's probably planning on hanging up the dust mop and moving into the mansion." Someone said.

"Dan Waters deserves better than that." The coroner's wife said.

They all knew she happened to have two spinster sisters that she would shove Dan's way the first chance she got.

At the mention of the Waters' housekeeper, Lottie listened intently. She said. "I've seen her, yes. She brought in a few of Miriam's old garments the other day. A very nice young lady, not at all the tawdry type...And simply thrilled that Miriam was returning. "

"I've seen her too." Another woman commented. "She and Dan Waters laughing together in the back garden when they thought no one was watching."

"There is nothing wrong in sharing a laugh with one's employer." Agnes answered. "I really don't see why we are even discussing this idle gossip."

"We understand your feelings Agnes you've lost a dear friend," the coroner's wife said grabbing her purchase.

Benjamin finally felt like his expertise was being appreciated. On the theory that two sets of eyes are better than one, Charles had asked that he accompany him to the opium den at the Wo Sing Café. He was part of the investigation.

"They do a brisk business selling Chop Suey and such, but it's the opium den in the basement that brings in the majority of their revenue." Charles told him as they walked into the café.

"There's no law against anyone squandering their lives away in an opium induced stupor, I suppose." Benjamin answered.

"You!" Charles said to the young man who scurried back and forth from the kitchen to the café.

"Yessir?" The man asked eyeing the two men cautiously.

"We want to go to the basement."
"Only storage down there, sir."

"Now that just isn't so!" Charles said. "We know full well you folks are providing opium down stairs and we want a look."

"I will see." The waiter said running to the kitchen. He returned moments later, followed by an elderly Chinese man.

"Why do you want to look in the basement, sir?" The old man asked.

Charles explained who he was and quickly added that he meant to cause no problem for the café or the opium den. "We are looking for someone who may have been involved in the recent murder."

The man grimaced. "Come this way then."

They crept down a narrow stone stairwell. The basement's ceiling was barely high enough for men of Charles and Benjamin's height. They ducked as he followed the man across the room's dirt floor. Two lanterns hung on the rock wall. The eerie blue flame of the opium smokers' pipes flickered across the basement, casting ominous shadows. Benjamin inhaled the sickly sweet aroma of opium wafting through the air. No mistaking that smell. Men and women lolled in spaces no larger than berths on a train. Each was lost in an opium-induced dream world.

They walked the narrow pathway between the berths eyeing each occupant intently.

As they climbed the stairs, Benjamin turned to look down. A group of people were huddled in a dark corner happily sucking their pipes. He hadn't seen them before. It couldn't be! And yet, as he watched the people focused only on their drug, he was certain that it was.

Thirty Two

The parlor was warmed by the afternoon sunshine that sparkled through the open lace curtains. A hollow stillness hung over the Silver Window.

Charles settled on a velvet settee and watched as Rose ushered Louise and Bridget into the parlor.

"I see you're back with the man who mistreats you Bridget." He said.

Her slender hand instinctively flew to her face. "No" She yawned. "This is a different man…anyway what business is it of yours?" She asked plopping on one of the wing back chairs across from him.

Charles looked at Louise who stood in the middle of the room. Her thick red hair was wildly tousled. She stared vacantly at the window as if looking for a way to escape. He waited until she sat down and then asked, "Louise, tell me again about Mary and the dial."

She stared at him blankly. "Dial? I--I don't know about that. It was too scary for me. Talking with all those dead people! Mary was the one who played with it all the time."

"What about you Bridget? Did you play with the dial?"

"We all did from time to time." She looked furtively around the room and dropped her voice to a whisper.

"Usually it was just Mary and me. But Wing Li and Rose liked to use the dial too. Only they didn't want Maude to know."

"Why didn't you tell me this the last time we talked?"

Bridget shrugged sullenly. "There was no need for me to."

He glanced at Louise who'd fallen asleep where she sat. "Louise!"

She sat up. "Uh huh?"

"Do you know who killed Mary?"

"No!" She gasped, fully awake.

"And what about you Bridget? Do you know who killed her?"

"How should I know?" She asked.

"I think you both know who the killer is, and you're just too scared to tell me."

"That's a lie!" Bridget exclaimed, jumping out of her chair. "I'd tell if I knew!"

Louise sobbed loudly. "Bridget, if you know tell him!"

When the tirade ended Charles watched them closely and asked if they knew anyone who wore ruby and diamond earrings. "What sort of earrings?" Louise asked springing from the sofa.

"Very expensive earrings." Charles answered.

"Is it a ruby with a lot of diamonds around them?" She asked.

"Yes. Have you seen such a pair?"

"I did!" Bridget said. "Mary was wearing some fancies like that the other night."

"Were they like this?" Charles asked holding the

earring out to her.

She grabbed it from him and examined it closely. "This looks like it could be...where did you get it?"

"Near the dead woman's body." Charles said.

Louise stared at the earring and fell to the floor screaming. "I don't want to die, Bridget! Oh no! We're all going to die. Please Bridget!"

"No one's going to die Louise." She snapped.

"Someone already has." Charles reminded her calmly. "Louise will you go get Rose and Wing Li?"

When she was gone Charles said. "Bridget, if you know who killed Mary you must tell me."

Fear fell across her face. "I don't. Honestly I don't."

Louise and Bridget returned with Rose and Wing Li.

"Thank you ladies, now if you will excuse us, I've some things I want to discuss with Rose and Wing Li."

Watching them walk from the room, something struck his memory and was gone.

"I'd like you two to know that I am about ready to make an arrest in this case." He said

Wing Li chuckled. "This is good news Mr. Bowling. At least there will be some justice for Mary. Now I suppose you'll leave us alone."

"I don't believe you!" Rose said. "If you were ready to arrest someone you'd have already done so."

"Be quiet Rose!" Wing Li hissed.

She turned on him. "How dare you speak to me like that. Who do you think you are?"

He smiled at her and asked. "Would you like Mr.

Bowling to arrest one of us for this murder?"

She sank down on the chair next to him. "You know full well we didn't kill Mary."

Wing Li grinned at Charles. "So which of us is to be arrested?"

"Neither of you at this point," he held out the earring. "However I would like to know if you recognize this."

Wing Li grabbed for it. And holding the earring so that it flashed in the sunlight he said. "A fine sparkling trinket, but I've never seen it before. What about you Rose?"

Rose stared at the earring a long while as if trying to remember something. "Yes. I saw one of the girls wearing a pair of earbobs similar to this. But I can't remember who it was. It may have been Bridget. No, wait a minute. I think it was Mary. Or was it Nora? No, I believe it was Bridget."

"You are certain this belonged to Bridget?" Charles asked.

"She may have stolen them for all I know. Why does it matter?"

Ignoring her, Charles asked. "Do either of you remember a lady coming to the house to see Mary?"

Rose and Wing Li exchanged glances. "Yes." Wing Li" replied. "But we don't know who she was."

"Why is that?" Charles asked.

"Because she concealed her identity by hiding behind widow's weeds." Rose explained. "At first I thought Mary was talking to herself so I went out to bring her in the house. They seemed to be friendly enough so I came back in. Then I heard them screaming at each other and Wing Li and I ran out to break up the fracas."

"They were scratching at each other like angry tigers." Wing Li agreed. "The lady's hat and veil were in tatters by the time the two gentlemen escorted her back to the coach."

"Mary was sobbing so loudly I was afraid she'd wake the house." Rose added.

"When was this?" Charles asked.

"The day before Mary…The day before Mary was sent away." Rose said.

"That would also be the day before she was murdered." Charles said absently.

"Where's Miss Banning?" Charles asked.

Rose's expression changed. Wing Li gasped. Finally he said, "Maude is very ill at this time."

"May I see her if only for a moment?" Charles asked.

"No!" He snarled. "You may not."

Charles stood. "I will accept that for now. But the next time I want to speak with her, I will arrest anyone who prevents me from doing so. Do you understand?"

Wing Li nodded silently.

"When I return, I shall be arresting the murderer."

"We didn't kill her!" Rose gasped. "Why should we?"

Wing Li looked directly at Charles. "While you're wasting your time on us Mr. Bowling, the real killer is still free."

Thirty Three

Enjoying the last late afternoon shreds of sunlight, Chief Dolan propped his feet upon his desk. He surveyed passersby on the sidewalk and willed the day to move faster. Glancing across the street, he saw Maude Banning coming straight for the office.

She angrily stomped through the door and sat in the chair nearest him. "We need to talk Farin."

"What's on your mind Maude?" he asked lighting a cigar.

"It's that assistant of yours. He's bothering the girls with all his questions and his visits." She inched her chair closer to him. "And I mean for it to stop."

Dolan smiled. "He's investigating the murder of one of your gals. It looks to me like you'd want him to find out who killed her."

"I do. But I'm damn tired of him coming around scaring everyone."

The Chief poured himself a saucer of coffee. "Care for a cup?" He asked.

She shook her head. "I'll be honest with you Farin. Our friendship demands at least that much. Last year I started using opium as a way to ease the pain of my rheumatism and before I realized it, I was like all the others who wile away their lives in the dens. I was addicted to the stuff. I tried to keep it a secret. But it's been an uphill battle for me. Thankfully I had Rose and Wing Li to help me. With their help and friendship, I'm free of the habit. I'm still suffering from its effects. While I've been unable to take care of things they've taken over and done a fine job. Now for some reason, it seems that Mr. Bowling has it in his mind to harass them and the girls almost daily."

Dolan looked at her closely.

"Charlie wasn't trying to harass anyone at your place Maude. He's like a hound with a bone when it comes to his investigations."

"I don't want to have to speak to Judge Minter or Senator Harris. But, if I should, you know as well as I, that it will ruin young Bowling's future aspirations. I am not an unreasonable woman. But I promise you, I will speak with both the judge and the senator the very next time he comes around bothering anyone at the Silver Window. "

The threat was real and powerful.

"Charlie's a fine young man Maude. It would be a shame to ruin him over something like this. Let me talk some sense into him."

Satisfied, Maude stood. "I need to get back."

"You best get back to bed. You're pale as a ghost." He smiled and took her hand. "Now don't you worry over young Charlie's enthusiasm. I'll see that he doesn't bother you again."

A MOTHER LODE OF MURDER

Thirty Four

Charles angrily paced back and forth.

"Every trail leads back to the Silver Window Chief. Why am I not being permitted to follow it?"

His arms akimbo, Dolan looked out the plate glass window. "I been Chief here in Virginia City more years than I care to think about Charlie…and part of that is not stepping on the toes of the powerful."

"Maude Banning has something to hide. Otherwise she wouldn't have made such a demand." Charles said. "She knows I am getting close—"

Dolan whirled. "Make no mistake about it boy. She's a powerful woman who whispers into the ears of the state's richest men…Can you say the same?"

Charles contemplated Dolan. Until this day he never realized how old the man was getting. He'd put on weight. His belly hung over the waist of his trousers. His shoulders sagged. And his once silvery salt and pepper hair was mostly white.

. "So you're telling me that Maude Banning has enough power to thwart a murder investigation?"

"I wouldn't call it thwarting Charlie. More like forcing you to stop looking for the killer at her bawdy house."

They silently watched as morning people hurried up and down C. Street. Ladies, with their full shopping baskets carefully walked along the sidewalk with their children tagging along after them, miners rushing to work or home, professional men chatting with each other as they made their way to the bank, the law office or the doctor's office. And in the street the endless stream of carriages coaches and horses.

When the sun went down the noise would intensify and a different crowd would come out to rule these sidewalks, a rowdier crowd, a thirstier crowd. And while they slaked their thirst in one saloon after another, tempers flared. Minor disagreements could turn violent in a flash. Then Charles, or another special officer, would step in to settle the issue before anyone was killed. Sometimes they were too late. The slower of the two gunfighters would lie dead in the street. More business for the undertaker; the crowd would move on. The show was over, until the next time. Vendors with their torches that lit up the night would once again loudly proclaim the benefits of their wares whatever they might be. Tooth powders, miracle cures, and countless tasty snacks like Cornish pasties, egg rolls, or jerky, all could be found along the streets at night.

Charles loved the vibrancy that was Virginia City, as much as Dolan did. But he would not happily push a murder investigation under the carpet just to satisfy Maude's wealthy clients. "So what do you want me to do exactly Chief?"

"I want you to be careful of whose toes you step on Charlie." Dolan sighed plopping on his chair. "And if you are, I can guarantee you this job is yours when I retire."

"How am I supposed to do that when I don't even

know who it is that I've upset?"

"Wellsir, you got Maude in a huff and like I already told you, she has some powerful friends."

"Martin Harris carries some clout in this town and I seriously doubt that he is one of them."

Dolan threw his head back and laughed uproariously. "Don't worry about him too much. He's nothing but a puppet no how." He was suddenly pensive. "Do yourself a favor Charlie and don't go back down there to the Silver Windows for a long while."

"But that is where the murderer is. So that is where my investigation should be centered."

"Look somewhere else. Just remember that most of these politicians are full of more hot air than a bull at green corn time. And they're a powerful bunch. Best just to let it be for now."

Charles poured himself a cup of coffee. In spite of himself he smiled at what Martin's reaction might be, had he heard the chief refer to him as a puppet.
"There is the possibility that Mary had stumbled onto one of Rose's sordid secrets and she killed her before she could tell anyone else."

"Why would Maude protect Rose if she's a killer?" Dolan asked. "She'd have no reason to."

"Because she's in love with Rose."

Dolan roared with laughter. "Maude isn't any more in love with that woman than I'm sweet on a rattlesnake!" His body shook with laughter. "You ought to be writing those dime novels, Charlie."

"When I told you what was being said about their unnatural friendship you said everyone in town knew about that." Charles countered.

"Maude is no one's fool. She knows how to get what she wants. Always has. She and Rose have been friends since before gold was discovered in California. Wagging tongues don't bother either of them one bit." He contemplated Charles' puzzled expression and smiled. "Charlie you got to learn the difference between gossip and fact."

"I ascribe to the old saw, 'where there's smoke there's fire'" Charles said defiantly.

"Then mayhap it was Hanlon that killed his wife." Dolan said.

"No."

"Why not?" Dolan asked pouring coffee in his saucer.

"He stood to gain nothing. And he's the sort that always wants to gain."

"Her rich sister is sure better off with Mary dead isn't she?" Dolan asked.

"She is Chief. But I hardly think she would be out in the canyon at that time of night. Much less murder someone."

"You never know what another human being will do." Dolan said. "I've seen mothers murder their own children just so they can chase after some man who doesn't want the bother. Had a man over in the jail once that killed his old mother so he wouldn't have to take care of her no more. I'm telling you Charlie people will sometimes fool you."

"You have my word Chief. I'll stay away from the Silver Window unless it's absolutely necessary." Charles assured him. "But I think the murder is somehow connected to the place, and in a strange way that damn dial that talks with the dead, as well."

Dolan laughed. "Talkin' with the dead is a cock and bull story if ever I heard one."

Thirty Five

After dinner Charles announced "I've got a surprise for you. I spoke with Mrs. Lloyd and she is coming tonight to conduct a private séance for us."

"When?" Sarah asked.

"She should be here anytime."

Lottie looked up from her mending. "What a wonderful idea dear. Maybe she will make contact with Mary Hanlon. She might even tell us who killed her."

"No Aunt Lottie." He chuckled. "I doubt that. I asked her to come so that we might conduct an experiment of our own."

"Who are we going to attempt to reach then?" Agnes asked. "Can we choose anyone? Whoever we wish to talk with?"

"Not exactly." Charles said. "Therese had an interesting theory. The more I thought it over, the more I thought she might be on to something. Our murderer might have killed Mary for something he believed the spirits had told her."

"This assumes the murderer believes in the dial's ability to communicate with the dead." Benjamin said.

"Or Mary Hanlon's ability to discover his secrets." Lottie suggested.

"Don't you need thirteen people for a séance?" Sarah asked. "I think you do."

"I have already told Mrs. Lloyd that there is only going to be six of us and she seems comfortable with that number." Charles said.

"So what are we supposed to do?" Therese asked. "Call out the names of anyone we know is dead?"

"I don't believe for a minute that we will be communicating with the dead tonight. I want to know how easily the dial can be manipulated and can it be made to spell out certain words." Charles explained as the doorbell rang.

Mrs. Lloyd daintily wiped her shoes and stepped nervously into the foyer. "Mr. Bowling, I apologize for being late." She stammered, "a personal matter of great importance."

"I hope it is nothing serious." Charles said, helping her to remove her heavy woolen cloak.

"Oh nothing like that." She smiled demurely. "My cat decided it was time to present me with four new kittens."

A cat lover in spite of the havoc with his sinuses, Charles smiled. Another reason to like Mrs. Lloyd.

The spiritualist wore a black taffeta dress that rustled when she moved. On her head was a tall black felt hat trimmed in black lace and wispy bottle green feathers. A black beaded shawl was carelessly slung over one shoulder.

She followed Charles into the parlor and smiled as he introduced her to the others. She quickly assumed the role of expert and explained the intricacies of a séance and the workings of the dial. Afterwards, he handed her two silver dollars, which she promptly tucked into her reticule.

"Ordinarily," she told them. "I would not even consider conducting a séance with less than thirteen. But Mr. Bowling has explained that this is meant to be an informal séance, so I have agreed. "

That and the two silver coins, Benjamin thought with a wry smile. He studied her face and realized she was much older than he had first thought. Standing this close to Mrs. Lloyd, and in this light, far more lines and wrinkles were revealed on her face than he'd seen from his tenth row seat at Piper's.

Her gloved hands trembled as she pulled several candles and an earthenware bowl from her large knitted satchel. "Would you be so kind as to fill this with water and place it on the table with the candles surrounding it?" She asked Lottie. Then to the others, she said. "It is always a good idea to have fresh cut flowers at the séance table. The spirits are drawn to the floral scent. Unfortunately it is too late in the season for them."

"Might we simply open a bottle of perfume?" Benjamin suggested.

The spiritualist wrinkled her nose in distaste. "Oh my goodness no. That would never do. The spirits would certainly know the difference."

"Humph!" Benjamin said. "We certainly wouldn't want to offend the spirits."

Mrs. Lloyd glared at him. "I would hope not sir!"

"Where might one buy a dial here in town?" Agnes asked.

"They would have to either purchase it from me or my associate, Mrs. Edwina Darlington." She thought a moment. "Or perhaps even a traveling salesman."

"Mrs. Darlington is the lady who introduced you at Piper's?" Benjamin asked.

"Yes that was she." She said placing the dial on the table. "Shall we be seated?"

They took their places around the big mahogany table. The flickering candles reflected in the water giving the room an ominous quality. Mrs. Lloyd pulled her black leather gloves off and looked at each of them solemnly. "Please join hands."

They did as they were told. "We shall call the spirits and then direct the dial to answer us." She said.

"We ask that only good and loving spirits kindly respond to us this evening. We are seeking any positive spirit who wishes to guide us, or to give us a message. If you wish to speak to us spirit, please do so."

Silence. "Everyone please touch the dial. I am sensing that one of us is a nonbeliever."

Benjamin shrunk from her accusatory stare. At least she was astute enough to realize that he didn't believe this nonsense for one minute.

"Oh! I see. I see that someone here has recently

lost a loved one." She exclaimed.

"It's Miriam." Agnes cried. "I knew she would come to us."

"Let us ask the dial to spell out the name, shall we?" The spiritualist said. "Please spirit, what is your name?"

The dial's pointer moved easily to the letters M--A--R--Y.

"Mary Hanlon! It's her!" Sarah shrieked.

"Is that your name spirit?" The spiritualist asked. The pointer did not move.

"We beseech you, speak to us!" She coaxed.

Benjamin squirmed impatiently in his seat. He'd had enough of this silliness and was anxious to get back to *War and Peace.*

"Spirits we are seeking someone to guide us." Once again the pointer remained motionless.

Mrs. Lloyd finally sighed. "I'm afraid the spirits are not willing to communicate with us any further this evening." She blew out the candles and the séance was concluded.

"One more question before you go Mrs. Lloyd." Charles said. "Do you recall having made contact with a group of miners that were trapped in the Yellow Jacket?"

She froze, suddenly unsure of herself. "I believe it was Edwina, Mrs. Darlington, who contacted their spirits."

When she was gone Benjamin said, "Interesting, but I don't see how this brings us any closer to catching the killer."

Charles explained, "I nudged the pointer to spell out

the word Mary. So it's just as I thought. Someone could easily have manipulated Mary's dial to spell out whatever words they wanted her to read."

"The killer?" Lottie asked.

"No. But I think the message spurred him into action."

Thirty Six

Mrs. Darlington's shop was next door to one of the larger Chinese laundries. When Charles walked in Mrs. Darlington looked up from her mending and smiled. She was alone in the shop except for a bright yellow canary that sang happily in its wicker cage. Age had affected her differently than it had her friend Lucinda Lloyd. Mrs. Darlington was still an attractive woman. The vestiges of youthful good looks were apparent in her smooth skin, twinkling blue eyes and curly thick iron gray hair. "May I help you sir?" She asked, placing her sewing on a small counter.

He introduced himself and she listened intently while he explained what he needed. When he finished speaking, she nodded and wiped her hands on her apron. "If you'll come with me I'll see if I have a record of that sale." She said.

He followed her to the back room of her tiny shop. The room had been given over to her sewing and there was barely space to move. Two bare mannequins stood near a sewing table that was covered with a swath of purple velvet. Stacks of colorful calico were everywhere. "Please excuse this clutter." She murmured pulling a leather bound book from under the sewing table. She thumbed through it nervously. As she did so yellowing pages fell from the book. "Ah yes. Here it is." She pointed a stubby finger at a scrawled notation, and said "Mary Hanlon two dollars for a dial."

"Do you make these dials yourself?" Charles asked.

She bowed her head a moment as if pondering whether to tell him anything. Finally she looked at him and said. "No. I order the small ones from a company in Illinois and the larger ones come from New York."

"I didn't realize they came in different sizes." He said.

She laughed happily. "Oh yes Mr. Bowling. The dial Lucinda brought to your home was a small one. I seriously doubt that she could lug a dial around the city." At the thought of her friend toting a dial, she laughed again "The large dial," She finally said. "Is too big and cumbersome for anyone living in rented lodgings. Here, come over here and see for yourself." She pulled several piles of yardage from what he at first thought was a long narrow table. "This is a dial." She said. "The sitter sits here and holds onto the pointer, then asks the spirits for guidance. See how each letter of the alphabet is represented on the round dial there?"

He nodded. "Like a clock.' He said. This was not something either Mrs. Lloyd or Mary Hanlon could carry around.

"The sitter is required to write down the spirit's replies one letter at a time.... Unless the spirit merely moves the dial to the word yes or no." She explained.

He lifted a corner of the dial. Maude Banning would have had a difficult time tossing this contraption out of the Silver Window.

She replaced the fabric covering the dial. "So Mrs. Lloyd and I sell the small dial to anyone with limited space."

"Does it work as well as this?" Charles asked pointing to the dial.

"Absolutely!" She assured him.

"May I ask you, how well did you know Mary Hanlon?" Charles asked.

She fidgeted with her hair. "She was a customer of course. I realize she went to work in one of the bawdy houses up the road there, but she was always such a nice person."

"Why did she buy a dial?"

"To speak with the spirits naturally.

"I meant how did she come to hear of it?"

"How does anyone hear of the spirit realm? She was very interested in spirit communication. I believe she had the potential to become a very gifted medium. When she lived up on the Divide she used to come to our séances and prayer circles regularly. That was when her husband was still alive."

"Were you acquainted with her husband?"

She frowned. "No. I only saw him a few times when he picked her up after a séance ...After he was killed she came around once or twice. Then she just stopped coming altogether. Someone told me she'd gone to work in one of the bordellos. "She looked into his eyes. "It was a terrible thing that happened to her, Mr. Bowling. I certainly hope you catch the person who is responsible."

"I plan on it." He said. "Do you happen to remember her husband's name offhand?"

"Why yes. It was the same as my youngest brother, Joseph. Joseph Hanlon."

"Did Mary and her husband get along?"

She chuckled. "Well of course an outsider never really knows these things, do they? They seemed to be very much in love. Yes, a happy marriage I would say…Poor thing. She just fell apart after he was killed."

Charles decided against telling her that Joseph Hanlon was very much alive. He also saw no point in repeating what the bartender at Jack Murphys had had to say about the Hanlons' happy marriage. "As you say an outsider never knows these things." He said.

"At least Mary had none of the bruises some of the wives in this city continually sport. " She pushed a strand of stray hair from her eyes. "Some of these men ought to be arrested for beating on these poor women the way they do…And I can tell you that they aren't all poor miners either."

Charles thought of the ugly bruises on Bridget's face and nodded. "I agree with you, it is a serious problem. But so many of them have children to feed and nowhere else to turn." He explained. "Without their husband's earnings--"

"I am well aware of that Mr. Bowling!"

It was obvious that this was a subject she felt strongly about. Charles decided it was time to talk about something else. "Do you if you know a man by the name Wing Li?" He asked.

Mrs. Darlington's demeanor changed. The twinkling blue eyes turned icy and her smile faded.

She was suddenly on the defensive. She stepped away from him and stood with her arms akimbo.

"May I ask why that is of any concern to you?"

This woman was not as open and friendly as he'd first supposed.

"Please don't forget that I am trying to solve the murder of someone you once knew, Mrs. Darlington. I asked the question because you were both acquainted with Mary Hanlon." His tone softened; now he would see if he had been right in his guess. "And you were also seen arguing with him outside Wo Sing's Café."

"I detest that despicable evil man…. All right! Yes I met him at Wo Sing's the other day."

"And why was that?"

"His youngest son married my cook's daughter. Everything seemed so storybook perfect." She stopped. "It's a long drawn out story. And trust me it would have nothing to do with your investigation--- Unless you're investigating a young couple that returned to China."

Thirty Seven

Jack Murphy's Saloon was busier than usual. Smoke and noise filled the air. To Charles' disappointment, the piano player was in his corner busily plunking out a melody of carefree tunes.

If the bartender recognized him he gave no indication. "What'll it be gents?" He asked smiling widely.

"Two beers." Charles said, and turning to Benjamin he asked. "I wonder if Mrs. Darlington knows Hanlon is still alive."

"If she doesn't she soon will."

The bartender slapped the foaming overfilled glasses of beer down in front of them. "What do you make of this weather, gents?"

"Cold as hell would be if it ever froze over!" Benjamin snorted. "I'm already tired of it"

"Yessir thems my sentiments." He swabbed the bar with a stained towel. "I shoulda stayed in Sacramento."

"Do you remember telling me about Joseph Hanlon?" Charles asked.

The bartender stared at him. Recognition spread across his face, followed by a scowl. "Yeah I remember you now." He snarled. "Asking about how Hanlon died."

"Hanlon's not dead." Charles said finishing his beer. "I saw him just the other day."

"He's dead I tell you. All the fellers was talking--" He glared at Charles. "Are you sure 'bout this mister?"

"Sure as I'm sitting here." Charles assured him.

"He musta been trying to beat me outta his bar tab. Why else would he ask them to tell me he was a goner?" The bartender smirked.

"He was also trying to run from his wife and his lady friend." Benjamin laughed.

The bartender turned to the spigot and refilled their glasses. "Lady friend? I don't believe that.

Mary was the only woman he ever talked about." He said slapping the glasses on the bar.

"You never saw him with any other woman?"

"No sir. He always came in with his friends or by himself. "

"You know anything about Mary Hanlon?" Benjamin asked.

"All's I know I already said. She liked to drink and she worked over at the Silver Window." He looked directly at Charles. "I told you 'bout her."

"Yes you did." Charles agreed.

When the bartender went to the other end of the bar, Benjamin said, "I still say it's that Wing Li you ought to be looking at."

"I can't do that. The chief has ordered me to stay away from the Silver Window."

Benjamin thought a moment. "Then grab him on the street. He's always running errands for Maude Banning—at the drugstore every day almost."

Their glasses empty, they headed for the door. "Mister! Will you do me a favor?" The bartender called to Charles.

"What's that?" Charles asked.

"Next time you see Hanlon tell him to get his ass in here and pay his bar tab."

Thirty Eight

The next morning Charles took Benjamin's advice and positioned himself outside of the drug store and waited.

He was just about ready to head back to the police station when he saw Wing Li approaching.

"Good morning Wing Li." He said in feigned cheerfulness.

Wing Li scowled. "You are to leave us be, Mr. Bowling."

Charles gently took hold of the collar of Wing Li's Hanfu jacket. "Now that's where you're mistaken. I may not be permitted at the Silver Window, but I can damn sure speak with you when I see you on the streets."

"I've nothing to say to you."

"In that case I will make it a point to see you somewhere else today or tomorrow or the day after. One way or the other we're going to talk."

Wing Li shrugged. "I'm in a hurry. Maude need's her medication, so make it quick."

"About Mary Hanlon," Charles said. "And I want you to think hard about this. Have you any thoughts on who might have killed her?"

"None whatsoever. Mary was a kind person who drew evil and bad things to herself. You see it resulted in her death."

"Odd that you're the only person who's had

anything nice to say about Mary Hanlon,"

"Mary, she wasn't like others. They couldn't understand the goodness in her." Wing Li said.

"So people at the Silver Window lied about her?"

Wing Li's expression was guarded. "I don't participate in gossip Mr. Bowling."

"We are not gossiping here. I am trying to find the man who killed her."

"And you are absolutely certain it was a man?" Wing Li asked sullenly."

Charles ignored the question. "I was told that you and Rose both left the house on the night of the murder. Why?"

"Bridget." Wing Li scoffed. "One of the evils that Mary drew to herself. If anyone at the Silver Window killed Mary, it was Bridget. She is without human emotions. Did she tell you that she was out that night as well?"

"I'm asking if you were away from the Silver Window."

"Of course I was. I am employed there, but I don't live there Mr. Bowling. I have my own family and responsibilities to take care of. "

. "Do you know anything about Mary's and Mrs. Darlington's friendship?"

The question startled Wing Li. He glanced furtively at the street. "Why should I?

"You had no knowledge of their friendship?"

"They weren't friends." Wing Li chortled. "Edwina Darlington is yet another of those evils that Mary pulled into her life."

"Do you mean her séances and her use of the

dial?"

"I am talking about Mary's husband, Joseph Hanlon." He smirked at Charles. "Ah, yes. I can see by your expression that you knew nothing of the romance between Edwina and Joseph Hanlon."

"How do you know this?" Charles asked. The absurdity of the well-educated Mrs. Darlington having a relationship with the foolish, unkempt Joseph Hanlon was almost laughable.

Wing Li shuddered. "When she first came to the Silver Window Mary told us that her husband was dead and she was not sorry. She said he'd been carrying on behind her back with Edwina Darlington. The romance had only come to light after his death. I don't think Edwina realized that Mary knew of the indiscretion. "

"Did she mention Mrs. Darlington in connection with her spirit communication?"

"Only that she believed she and Edwina could talk to the dead."

"Did she tell you about a woman named Dora?"

"Who is that?"

"Joseph Hanlon's current lady friend."

"Current? The man's been dead for some time."

"I'm afraid not."

Wing Li laughed merrily. "Wait until Edwina finds out. I wouldn't want to be in his shoes. She can kick up a devil of a temper tantrum. Make her mad enough and she'll throw anything she can get her hands on at you. "

Charles studied him carefully. He'd almost decided Wing Li was an accomplished liar when he remembered Mrs. Darlington's anger at being asked if she was acquainted with him.

"Do you think Rose had something to do with Mary's death?"

"Rose couldn't kill anyone. "

"And neither, I suppose, could you." Charles said.

"There sir, you are mistaken." Wing Li bragged. "Given the right set of circumstances I could kill in an instant."

Charles looked at him thoughtfully. "Yes, I believe you could."

"But I did not kill Mary." Wing Li said, turning from Charles.

Thirty Nine

The stage for Sacramento left the International Hotel promptly at seven. Benjamin was on a mission. If he were successful they would have their killer.

As the coach made its way down Geiger Grade he gazed out the window. Hopefully the light rain would keep down the dust. He rested his hand on his holster, ready if a robber should show up.

He settled back in the coach. It would be a long journey to Monterey.

A dense fog rolled in off the bay filling the air with the smell of fish. The fishing fleet was in and street was crowded with wives and cooks anxious to get down to wharf and the fleet's offerings. Benjamin's knees ached as he walked along Calle Principal. He'd almost forgotten how the damp salt air could penetrate right to the bones. Hopefully Pembrooke's Fine Jewelry would be his last stop in his quest for answers.

Hailed by competitors and comrades alike as the finest on the peninsula, Pembrooke's shop was far smaller than he expected. An elderly man sat behind the counter deeply engrossed in a book. At Benjamin's discreet cough he closed the book and set it on the counter. Pushing his reading glasses up to his forehead he asked, "May I be of assistance?"

"I hope so sir." Benjamin said placing the earring on the counter. "Did you make this?"

The old man grabbed his loupe and examined the earring closely. "Hmmm." he said as he turned it from one side to the other.

"I believe this is a design of mine. See there by the inset. See the O.P.? That's my initial. Oswald Pembrooke." He handed the loupe to Benjamin who saw nothing but squiggles.

"Can you tell me anything about the person who purchased it?" He asked hopefully.

The old man gently placed the earring down and contemplated Benjamin. "I'd have to look in my drawings and design books. And that might take several hours."

"It's very important." Benjamin assured him.

"Tell you what. I close at five. You come back then, bring a nice bottle of wine and we can go over the books together."

Benjamin looked at the old man. Lonely no doubt, and he did have information.

"I'll be back at five."

He returned with a bottle of wine under each arm. Smiling broadly, Oswald Pembrooke led him behind the counter to his back room. A workbench, two chairs, tools, magnifying glasses and stacks of leather bound notebooks filled the small room.

"First let's have a drink." Pembrooke said pulling two filmy glasses from under the bench. He deftly opened the bottle and poured their glasses full.

"I wondered if you'd come back or not."

Benjamin sipped his wine slowly. "As I told you earlier, this is a matter of utmost importance."

"What makes it so?" Pembrooke asked.

"I am investigating a murder case that took place in Virginia City." Benjamin explained. "This earring may play a crucial part in apprehending the killer."

Pembrooke poured himself another glass of wine. "Virginia City huh? I was there once. Didn't care for it one iota. Lots of folks getting rich up there in all that silver though. The place didn't suit me. Too much dust and wind. My god man, how do you keep yourselves from blowing away?"

"Yes it is considerably drier than here." Benjamin said kicking himself for bringing two bottles of wine. Oswald Pembrooke had a tendency to drift away from the subject at hand. The wine wouldn't help matters. "A question for you, Mr. Pembrooke. How did you know that I didn't intend to come back and rob you?"

Pembrooke laughed loudly. "Of what? Any fool knows this is merely where I take orders and design the jewelry. All of my precious stones are kept in a heavily guarded warehouse in Salinas."

"I see." Benjamin said. "Now about these earrings. Do you remember this particular design?"

Pembrooke stared at him a moment then smiled. "After you left I looked in the books and I found the design. I remember perfectly."

"The buyer's name?" Benjamin asked, straining to keep the excitement from his voice.

"It was a husband and wife. Here see for yourself." He handed Benjamin a crumpled receipt.

"She was with him?" Benjamin asked glancing at the receipt.

"Oh yes! Matter of fact the pattern was basically her idea. Some romantic design she'd seen in some San Francisco jeweler's window, I suppose. She drew me a sketch of what she wanted. Diamonds encircling a ruby with an intricate gold setting, good quality diamonds too…from the Kimberly Mines in South Africa and the pigeon blood rubies were Burmese from the Mogok Valley. Not cheap, no certainly not cheap. But she knew what she wanted. And he wanted her to have it. Such a nice couple. We shared a celebratory bottle of Pinot noir when they picked up all the earrings. "

"All the earrings?" Benjamin asked.

"Well yes. She wanted two identical pairs made. I suppose she was worried about losing one of them." He grinned at Benjamin. "Didn't you see that on the receipt? It says two pairs of earrings."

When the night was over Benjamin's head throbbed and his stomach felt queasy. He'd imbibed more wine than any sensible man should. But he had learned plenty in the process. Yes, there was something peculiar about those earrings. Benjamin thought as he stumbled down Alvarado toward the hotel.

Forty

Therese crept into the parlor and let her long slender fingers absently glided across the piano keys. This murder had nearly consumed them. Yet none of them were any closer to a solution than they'd been on the first night. She played the piano and contemplated the restrictions placed on women.

The world was such an unfair place for a female. Charles and Benjamin could go to the Silver Window, or any other place in the city for that matter, without fear of reprisals. If she were seen anywhere near a house of ill repute it would surely mean dismissal from her job at the school. Therese angrily pounded out a maudlin tune she remembered from childhood. If only she could get into the Silver Window. She would find out far more than Charles ever could.

She let her mind wander. There was one way. Yes, she would do it. But she would need help.

Sarah was more adventuresome than the others realized. Therese had discovered this side of her early on, and they had become fast friends. It didn't take Therese long to talk Sarah into helping her in her scheme that would surely shock the others. Sarah liked the idea and eagerly helped Therese in her plan of infiltrating the brothel.

As Therese made her transformation, Sarah stared in disbelief and said, "I can hardly believe this is you."

The metamorphosis was complete. Therese had taken the pins from her thick chestnut brown hair so that it tumbled down her back in shiny waves. On her face and lips was a dollop of bright pink rouge. Her dress was of bright purple taffeta onto which she'd sewn several rows of black Chantilly lace. "So you think I look the part?" She asked carefully examining her reflection in the cheval mirror.

"Oh yes! You certainly look like a trollop." Sarah laughed. "But are you sure this won't be dangerous?" "I would never forgive myself if anything happened to you."

Therese placed a comforting hand on the old woman's shoulder. "Not to worry. I was an excellent thespian in school."

Sarah scoffed. "This isn't school Therese. These people are the very dregs. They'd sooner--"

"I wouldn't do this if I didn't think that one of them is our killer. And I will be careful..."

The two conspirators carefully developed their plan. Next morning Sarah announced that Therese was too ill to come down for breakfast. After Charles left she sneaked around to the back window and helped Therese climb down the ladder, they'd placed the night before.

"Are you certain that you want to do this?" Sarah asked as Therese rearranged her dress.

"It's the only way I know to gather information that may help Charles catch this murderer."

The women shared a warm embrace and Therese hurried down Sutton St.

Her throat was dry and her heart pounded. Could she carry this off? Then after a moment's hesitation, she rang the doorbell. Rose opened the door and glared at her.

"Yes?"

Therese stammered the name Annie and her reason for being there. Without a word, Rose ushered her into the parlor. She glanced around the room. It was exactly as Charles described it. He'd cleverly neglected to mention the nude paintings, she smiled to herself.

Rose eyed her curiously. "Have a seat and tell me what brought you to the Silver Window, Annie."

Therese' heart lurched. She'd already been found out. No matter. She would keep up the charade. "My man's left me without money for the rent." She said, doing her best to mimic the manner of speech used by some of the women who came to the charitable society seeking help.

"I'm sure there are several places in town where you can earn enough to pay your lodging."

The old harridan was toying with her. She would toy back. "The man up at Jack Murphy's told me I'd be wasting my time coming' here. Said you only hire old women. And that you got no use for pretty ladies such as myself."

Rose's face turned crimson. She jumped up from the sofa, and demanded. "Who told you such nonsense?"

Therese coyly lowered her eyes. "I don't rightly recall his name. He was a nice gent though. Bought me a whiskey and--"

"It's not important. We've got room for you Annie, if you can obey the rules.

"I can." Therese said. "Oh yes I can obey the rules."

"I haven't told you what they are." Rose smiled.

"Well, what are they?"

"We will not tolerate any sneaking out at night. No holding back on the money. We keep half of everything you make. If a gentleman is especially impressed and gives you a nice extra gift, we expect to share with you equally. No holding back. You understand?"

Therese nodded. "No holding back."

"Your room and board is two dollars a day. We expect payment every Saturday."

"What if I don't make any money? I still have to pay room and board?"

"This is not a charity ward, of course you do. And if you don't pay, you're out." Rose threatened. "You'll sleep during the day. That may take some getting used to. But since the house is open from early candle-lighting to sun up there's no other time."

"Thank you ever so much Miss--?"

"Rose." She turned toward the hall. "Wing Li" She

yelled.

A stooped Asian man came running.

"Show the new girl to her room, please."

Therese silently followed him up the stairs to a vacant room filled with throwaway furniture. A tattered pink coverlet was haphazardly tossed across the bed. An iron bed table and a walnut dresser completed the room's furnishings. The walls were bare except for a small oval mirror.

"This is your room." Wing Li said. "Stay here until mealtime. Or time to go into the parlor." He turned back. "And keep this door closed."

She nodded and fell onto the bed. They believed her. When he was gone she looked out the window. In the distance she could see the church and the school and the Ducks and Deeks. She thought of Mary Hanlon, and wondered how many times she had looked out this very window at those same places. Therese closed the curtain and listened. Someone was softly knocking on her door.

"Who's there?" She asked.

"It's Louise, may I come in and meet you?"

Therese opened the door to a redheaded girl who smiled shyly. "Sorry if I disturbed you. Just wanted to come and say hello."

"Come in." Therese motioned to the bed. "Please won't you sit down?"

"I'm Louise" The redhead said falling onto the bed. She wore a red calico dress and pinafore. Her hair was coiled in a neat bun at the nape of neck. To Therese she looked like a schoolgirl rather than a habitué of a bawdy house.

"I'm Annie." Therese said.

The redhead stared at Therese deciding whether or not to trust her. Finally she lowered her voice and said. "I bet you think you've found a good place. And mayhap you have. But you better know that there's some bad people here in this place. So be careful. A lot of stuff that goes on here isn't nice. The woman who lived in this room before you was murdered."

Therese touched her head feigning shock. "Who killed her?" She asked.

"Why someone who lives here." Louise said nervously. "Didn't I just tell you to be careful?" She giggled.

There was another knock at the door. "Hello! Hello in there! May I come in?"

Louise was suddenly frightened. "Please don't say what I told you." She begged.

Therese assured the girl that she wouldn't and opened the door to another young woman.

"Oh Louise I might have known you'd be here." She laughed. Then taking Therese's hand she said, "I'm Bridget. My room's next door. "Her dark hair was swept back in a shiny thick plait and like Louise, she wore a bright calico dress and pinafore.

"I'm Annie. Louise and me just met…I'm hungry. When's supper?" Therese said.

Bridget's eyes darted from Therese to Louise. "It's at five." She dropped onto the bed. "Has Louise told you all about the dead woman that got murd--"

With a silent prayer that her thespian forbears

guide her, Therese jumped up angrily. "If you two doxies think you're gonna scare me off with some dead woman ghost tale, you got another think coming."

Bridget and Louise exchanged bewildered looks. Finally Bridget laughed. "We didn't aim to scare you. We were just trying to share some gossip is all."

She had only a day here at best. Therese needed to make good use of that time. "I don't like gossip." She said.

"Then I guess you don't want to hear how Rose and Wing Li are trying to take this place from Maude." Bridget teased.

Therese had to be careful. If she appeared overly anxious it might scare these two away. "All the same to me, but Rose did say that Maude is sick." She said.

Louise giggled. "She's always sick when the opium runs out."

Bridget laughed. "That's how they plan on taking the place Louise!" She stood and stared out the window. "With all the silver under this town you'd think there'd be plenty to go around. Enough to make a rich woman of me at least."

"Go on Bridget. You aren't ever going to be rich." Louise said.

Bridget whirled around. "Don't be so sure of it." She hissed.

Therese laughed. "Before you get to fighting one of you ought to tell me about that dead woman's ghost."

"There's no ghost Annie. Her name was Mary and

she lived in this very room. Somebody murdered her. Isn't that so Louise?"

Louise dropped her head and sobbed. "Why do you always scare me with that?"

Bridget laughed. "I'm not trying to scare you Louise, only saying what happened."

"Well I don't like it." Louise said. "So please don't say it no more okay?"

Bridget smiled cruelly. "Okay. But we know there's a killer amongst us don't we Louise?"

Louise ran from the room sobbing. Bridget turned to Therese. "Her conscience is bothering her again."

"You aren't saying it was her killed that woman Mary are you?" Therese asked.

"Could be I am. Could be I'm warning you to be careful of Louise." She ran for the door. "But maybe I'm just fooling with you Annie."

When she was gone, Therese fell onto the bed. Would poor Mary Hanlon's killer ever be caught? There was always the possibility that the crime would never be solved. She closed her eyes and shuddered at the thought. And in spite of herself, Therese drifted off to sleep.

Rose banged on the door. "Come to the parlor Annie," she called cheerily.

"What time is it?"

"Nearly ten now get a move on." Rose

responded.

Her stomach churned. She'd missed dinner. And it was well past her bedtime. What if someone should see me, she wondered. There could be no suitable explanation for being here. Only Charles and Sarah would understand. And Charles wasn't even aware that she was here tonight. She applied more rouge, tousled her hair and slowly walked downstairs to the parlor. A woman was playing a lively tune on the piano. Most of the men who lounged on the sofas were dressed in finery befitting Piper's Opera House. Thick cigar smoke hung in the air and assailed her nostrils.

She stepped behind a potted plant at the doorway and watched as the girls laughed and danced with the men. Louise sat on the lap of a man Therese recognized from Sunday's church services. Therese stepped back in panic. What if he should see me, she thought.

Someone tapped her on the shoulder and she jumped. "Annie! Why are you hiding out here in the hall?" Rose demanded.

"I'm scared." Therese said, wiping her hands through her hair. "I never worked in a bawdy before Mam."

Rose laughed. "That is forgiven tonight. Still I must warn you, you won't pay your room and board by hiding out here."

"Yes Mam."
Rose smiled at her and was gone.

At the far end of the parlor Bridget proposed a toast to the Comstock, and Therese turned to see her gulp a glass of champagne. "And here's to my special friend, Bryce!" Bridget giggled, pouring herself another drink. "He's a wonderful person indeed."

Determined to see who Bridget's *special friend* was, Therese stepped from behind the plant. Louise saw her. "There's the new girl everyone! Hey Annie, Come join the fun."

Therese turned and ran up the stairs, the sound of laughter echoing in her ears. She'd made a mistake coming here, she was ready to leave. Even if she should discover anything how would she explain that discovery?

Someone was sobbing in the large room at the end of the hall. Therese crept to the door and pressed her ear against it.

"Wing Li! How can you be so cruel to me?" A woman cried. "I have done nothing wrong. Rose, please. Please tell him that he is mistaken." She begged.

"We are not mistaken Maude" Wing Li snapped. "Rose and I forbid you to ever again--"

"No!" She howled. "Who are you to forbid me anything in my own house?"

"This is difficult on all of us." Rose said.

"I will not agree to your outlandish demands!"

"Very well, we'll leave you here to think the matter over." Rose said.

Therese raced back down the stairs to her spot behind the potted palm.

Bridget was sitting in a man's lap and laughing happily. Therese edged closer. There was something vaguely familiar about him. He stood and took Bridget's hand. They were coming right toward her. She quickly stepped back in the darkened alcove. Arm in arm they strode past her. As they ascended the stairs Therese covered her mouth to prevent herself from gasping out loud when she realized who was walking with Bridget.

Forty One

The Coombs were childless. Their dogs had always filled whatever parental instincts they might possess. Pedro a black and white mixed mutt was, they both agreed, the smartest dog they'd ever owned. He was also their favorite. Wherever they went, so went Pedro.

Mort Coombs bragged that his canine's bark was so deep and loud it could be heard from the Divide all the way down to Geiger Grade. True or not, Pedro was an excellent hunter. Invariably it was he who chased down and caught most of the jackrabbits that ended up in Mrs. Coombs' stew pot.

Mr. and Mrs. Coombs, their pack mule and Pedro were wandering in an area far from the city, near Flowery Mountain where the Sagebrush grew lush and thick. The Chinese wood gatherers hadn't discovered this secret cache so there was still plenty of thick stemmed old sagebrush stumps to cut and sell. Mort pulled the burlap bag off the mule's back and tossed it to the ground. And stooping over the bag, they cut the sagebrush stalks into thin pieces of stove wood that they would later wrap into tight little bundles of twenty and peddle all over town for six bits a bundle.

While *his parents* tossed their wood into the sack, Pedro grew restless. Not as old and tired as the mule, the dog sought adventure. He stood still, all his senses alive and at the ready. His pointed snout sniffed the breeze deeply while his eyes surveyed the landscape for the quick darting movements of a jackrabbit.

When he spotted the rabbit he sprang on his hind legs and gave chase without a backward glance at the Coombs. Laughing at the dog's eagerness, they continued with their task. And then Mort Coombs looked up just in time to Pedro race across the sagebrush and vanish.

"Pedro you worthless cur! Get back here."

From the distance came the deep yelping of a dog in trouble.

"Pedro my boy! Don't fret. We're coming" Mrs. Coombs called with more bravery than she felt.

"Pedro? Where in tarnation are you?" Mr. Coombs called. The dog continued yelping. "I think he might have fallen into a shaft." Mr. Coombs said to his wife. "One minute I saw him and the next he was gone."

The old woman's heart froze. "We gotta go find him, Mort! Come on now."

From where they stood, the shaft appeared to be no more than 20 feet deep. Their beloved Pedro could probably be rescued. Luckily he hadn't fallen into one of the shafts that went so deep into the earth he could never get out. Not knowing this, the dogs frightened whimpers rose up from the shaft.

"We'll need a windlass to save him. I'll get back to town and find some help." Mr. Coombs said to his wife who stood at the edge of the shaft and cried to the dog.

"You go on then. I'll stay here with Pedro."

While she waited, Mrs. Coombs cursed every miner on the Comstock for creating the shaft her pet had tumbled into.

When he'd rounded up some help, Mr. Coombs led the men back out into the canyon. At the shaft Mrs. Coombs told the doubtful men that Pedro was smart enough to jump into the large bucket. So they set the windlass across the shaft, turned the handle, slowly unwound the rope and attached bucket.

"Pedro jump in!" She called down into the shaft. "Come on my fine boy. You can do it."

The dog responded with a loud bark, but wouldn't get in the bucket. After three attempts they agreed that the only way to save the dog was for Mr. Coombs to go down in the bucket and get the dog himself. The old man nervously climbed aboard the bucket and was lowered down

As his eyes adjusted to the darkness he stepped out of the bucket and called out. "Come here Pedro." The dog leapt toward him, licking his face happily. "There, there my good boy. You're okay now."

Mr. Coombs looked around the shaft. "A few more feet and you'd been a goner for—"

The crumpled body of a woman lay close enough for him to touch. There would be no rescue for her. Her neck turned at an odd angle, her long hair fanned out from her head. "Oh my Lord…"

He crawled back into the bucket holding Pedro tightly.

"Get us up, now!" He yelled.

One of the men raced back to town and straight to the Police Station. Once again Charles and Chief Dolan found themselves listening to a tale that involved the discovery of a woman's body.

Dolan lit his cigar and surveyed the man who stood at his desk panting for breath. "You say Mort Coombs found her?"

"Yes sir."

"Did he say if she had fallen in or if--" Charles let his question drift off. Mort wouldn't have told this man anything except to fetch the police."

"Wellsir." Dolan said. "Looks like you better head out there, Charlie." He hesitated. "'Course if you need me."

"I'll handle it, Chief." Charles assured him.

Dolan grinned. "Then I'll just stay right here and do some paperwork."

Charles knew full well that this meant he would be snoozing at his desk unless otherwise disturbed.

Charles lit his lantern and was lowered into the shaft. Holding the light aloft, he swept it back and forth. The dead woman was lodged against the shaft's wall. A silver dagger had been thrust deep into her chest. Dark crimson stains spread across the bodice of her dress and cape. Whoever pushed her into the shaft had done so with the intention that her body would tumble down into oblivion.

He examined her torn and scraped leather gloves. She'd been alive when someone pushed her into the shaft. Mortally wounded, the woman instinctively grabbed for something to hold onto as she fell. The jutting ledge had stopped her descent and she'd died here, alone in the darkness. Charles brushed her thick hair aside and studied her face. Anger rose within him as recognition dawned.

This murder was connected to that of Mary Hanlon and he meant to find out how. And once he did that, he would have the killer.

Until this moment, he had believed that Rose and Wing Li murdered Mary to keep her quiet about Maude's addiction to opium. That also explained the two people the Coombs heard talking in a buggy on the night of the murder.

Benjamin's theory of a love triangle might not be so wrong after all. But the members of that triangle had just shifted. With the discovery of this body, the course of his investigation was altered. The killer would need to move fast. And he would have to move faster.

He lifted the dead woman into the bucket, and carefully covered her face with the blanket he'd brought down.

"Haul it up!" He yelled. "And mind you, do not remove that cover from her face!"

Back up top, Charles admonished the men. "No one, and I mean no one, is to speak of finding this body to a soul!"

He then sent one of them for the coroner, who he would order not to say a word to his gossiping wife.

Forty Two

Mrs. Darlington greeted him warmly. "I'll be with you in a moment, Mr. Bowling."

She finished with her customer and turned to Charles with a smile. "If you're here with any more questions, I've already told you everything I know about Mary."

"Except the truth."

"How dare you!" She bluffed. "Bothering law abiding citizens."

Then watching his face, she sagged against the counter and sighed. "It's Joseph isn't it? You know about Joseph and me."

"You lied to me, Mrs. Darlington."

She gasped. "I--well--that is. That isn't exactly something I'm proud of."

"So you and he were friendly?"

She smirked. "Oh I don't suppose someone your age can possibly understand. But I was lonely and vulnerable and he--"

"You did this even though he was married to your friend Mary?"

"I did say that I wasn't proud of myself." She said.

"When did the romance end?"

She bowed her head. "When he was killed."

Charles was going to enjoy telling her the truth. "There's something you should know...."

"And what's that?" She asked

"Joseph Hanlon isn't dead."

"That's impossible. I remember Mary was so distraught and--"

"He had a new woman in his life. And he wanted to escape both of you. So he and his friends concocted a story that coincided with the cave in."

She fell into her chair. "That dirty scoundrel! If I could get my hands on him right now, I'd choke the life out of him." She looked up, her eyes shining with fury. "Where is he?"

All the more reason, Charles decided not to tell her where to find her erstwhile lover.

"Did you know that Hanlon tried his hand at blackmailing Mary's sister?"

"What are you talking about?"

"Pardon me Mrs. Darlington. But it's incomprehensible, a lady like you, obviously well educated, and a man like Joseph Hanlon. "

"I had recently lost my own husband and--"

Her reasons were her own. Charles didn't need to hear them. Neither did he care to listen to a litany of excuses "Have you any idea how Hanlon lives?"

"He and Mary rented very nice rooms at the Morrow House."

"The man lives in filthy squalor." Charles shook his head in disgust.

"I guess his lifestyle has changed somewhat since his death." She smirked.

Charles left the shop, and crossed Mrs. Darlington off his list of suspects.

Forty Three

The evening crowd was milling about on the wooden sidewalks, ready for a night of revelry. Chief Dolan and Charles were still at the police station discussing the long day's events. Dolan pulled his chair to the stove and rubbed his fleshy hands together. "Here it is October and already my rheumatism is giving me fits! Dan DeQuille over at the Territorial Enterprise can make jest of it all he wants, but I tell you Charlie it's not easy getting old."

"I suppose not." Charles replied his mind preoccupied and not the least bit concerned with the state of the Chief's health.

The chief hunched his heavy frame nearer the stove's warmth. "Martin Harris had been here twice today, chomping at the bit. He wants to get in that courtroom and be the star of another trial." He smiled. "If it wasn't' for his father's money he'd be just another young lawyer. How long you figure he'll allow us to keep this dead woman a secret?"

Charles thought a moment. "I don't think we need to do that."

"Yeah?"

Charles sat down. "I have a couple of ideas, I just need the evidence."

Dolan laughed. "Ideas? Everybody's got ideas my boy. Young Harris will have both our hides if we hold up his strutting in a courtroom much longer." Rubbing his knees, he added. "I'm wondering if maybe this Hanlon and Mrs. Darlington didn't make up some tall tale to cover the murder of Mary."

"They had no reason for that. She didn't have a penny to her name."

"That Mrs. Bramwell is a very rich woman. Mayhap she hired the two of them to do away with the inconvenient sister."

"I'd say these two murders are connected somehow. And this would take Mrs. Bramwell out of consideration."

"No Charlie, I don't see that. One thing's for sure, we'd better be damn sure about who that dead woman is. Are you?"

"I have no doubt whatsoever."

"That's good enough for me." The Chief eased himself to his feet. "I'm for calling it a night. Tomorrow's another day."

Charles wasn't about to disagree, not tonight, With Benjamin gone he was anxious to get home to the ladies. Every one of them could handle a pistol as well as any man. He'd seen to that. Still he didn't like the idea of them all alone in the rooming house after dark.

They stepped out the door just as a horse came galloping down C. Street. A young man slid down from the horse, panting and nearly out of breath.

"Which of you gents is Bowling? "

"I'm Bowling."

"I gotta urgent message for you from Sally Swan up at the Barbary Coast."

The man stepped closer to Charles. "Sally she's dying. Consumption the doc says. She's not got long. Said to tell you she knows something 'bout a murder. Better come quick."

"You best go up then, Charlie." Dolan said wearily. A fast ride up to the Divide was the last thing he felt like doing tonight.

A bitter wind whipped across his face as he urged his horse up the hill. He doubted that Sally Swan knew anything that could help him make an arrest, but she'd summoned him to her deathbed and he would not be disrespectful and ignore her.

The same plump redhead bartender was at the bar when he raced into the saloon. She acknowledged him with an unsmiling nod and said, "She's in back."

Charles heard the wracking cough even before he stepped through the curtained door to find her lying in a narrow bed in the corner. "Miss Swan it's Charles Bowling." He said. "I understand you have something to tell me regarding Mary Hanlon's murder."

Sally slowly rose up on one elbow. Her ashen face resembled that of a skeleton. "Doc tells me I'm not long for this earth. I got the same cough that Mary had, the very same." Her words were punctuated by several loud barking coughs.

"I'm sorry." Charles said calmly.

She smiled weakly. "No need to be. You were a true gent to me, Mr. Bowling. And being as how I never forget a kindness, I'm fixing to tell you the truth of what I--" She coughed for several minutes.

When she finally stopped, Sally said. "The night before Rose sent me packing I heard something I been wondering about. I was tired and headed up to my room. I left my door ajar. So in case Rose or Wing Li needed me. "

She sat up propped herself against the wall. "Will you fetch me a glass of water?"

He poured her a large glass from the pitcher beside her bed and she continued. "I heard them talking. A man and a woman. I heard him say 'If you do as I say we can have it all.' Then she said something like, 'Twice! I don't want to kill anyone. We got enough' or something like that."

"Did you recognize the voices?"

"It was Bridget--- talking with Wing Li." She drained her water glass and fell back on the bed. "That's all I can tell you. Now leave me be. I got to make my peace here before--"

Charles thanked her gently and stepped back out to the bar. "How long?" He asked the bartender who busily ran a towel across the bar.

"The doctor didn't give her till morning."

While Charles was at Sally Swan's bedside, Lottie, Agnes, Sarah and Dan enjoyed a superb dinner prepared especially for Dan by Mrs. Noonan. The cantankerous cook had developed a soft spot for the lanky widower who praised her culinary skills and lavished her with compliments on her well-ordered kitchen.

The table was heaped with Dan's favorites. He needed to put some weight on his skinny frame all the women agreed. The subject was Miriam, as it often was whenever Dan was present.

"She had a lovely soprano voice." Sarah said solemnly remembering Miriam in the church choir. "Yes lovely." Agnes agreed. Dan smiled proudly. "There will never be another woman quite like Miriam."

"I understand that Dan. But in time you may fall in love and remarry. Men don't seem to fare as well as women do in these circumstances." Lottie said.

"Oh no!" He gasped. "Why would I marry again? There is no other quite like her in all the world. He smiled across the table at Agnes, who returned the smile. "She is so gifted; she designs her own clothing, and often designs her own jewelry as well." His face turned ashen. "Oh!" He sobbed, covering his eyes with his slender hands.

"Miriam was an altogether talented woman." Sarah agreed. Even as she spoke the words, Sarah realized they were lies. Lies told with no other purpose than to ease the widower's pain. What would the recipient herself make of all the lies, Sarah wondered. Miriam, who spoke only the truth, even if it offended, would no doubt be horrified to hear so many lies told about her.

After dinner they moved to the parlor with its

comfortable sofas and blazing fireplace. Sarah, with the help of Mrs. Noonan, prepared a tray for the bedridden Therese.

"How is she feeling?" Lottie asked as Sarah crossed the hall and headed for the stairs. "Perhaps I ought to pop in cheer her up and say hello."

Sarah froze in her tracks. "That would not be a good idea. She specifically said she wanted no one caring for her but me." She boasted. "You know how unreasonable she can be when she is under the weather?" She asked softening the blow to Lottie's good intentions.

"If she's very ill I could send Theodore's caretaker around to check and see how she's doing." Dan suggested.

"That isn't necessary." Sarah said. "I am quite capable of caring for her.

"Why Sarah, I didn't realize you had a medical degree." Dan teased.

She glared at him. "I don't and she's not that ill."

"Give her my regards."

After spending what she considered was enough time in Therese's room, Sarah returned to the parlor and found them playing cards.

"Her fever has subsided and she is sleeping soundly," She lied, picking up her needles and yarn. While she quietly absorbed herself with her knitting, Sarah's thoughts were on Benjamin. She would never admit it to another living soul, but she missed him.

Suddenly she remembered something someone had said earlier in the evening that didn't seem important at the time, but now… Sarah examined her knitting. To her dismay she realized she'd dropped a stitch rows down. It would take her awhile to repair the mistake. She was too tired to even bother with it tonight. She folded her knitting in the basket and decided she would talk with Charles in the morning.

"So you've found a buyer?" Lottie asked.

For the first time in days Dan smiled. "Oh yes isn't it wonderful? The agent of a wealthy widower from back east has approached me with his intent to purchase. The agent believes the home is exactly what his employer is looking for. He wants to come west to be nearer a brother who lives in Carson City."

"When will you be moving?" Agnes asked deftly dealing out cards.

"Very soon. The buyer wants to be in the house before winter sets in. We just need to finalize the deal"

Lottie threw down her winning hand to the consternation of the others. "Dan that's wonderful news for you, but you mustn't forget us. Promise me you won't"

"Of course I will never forget any of you. I shall miss all of you immensely."

Sarah glowered at them from the wing chair. At least Benjamin would have included her in the discussion, even with a caustic remark. "Miriam's memorial was very lovely." She said.

He stared at her. "Why Sarah, I thought you'd fallen asleep over your knitting."

The others chuckled and he joined in. Sarah seethed. She knew an adversary when she saw one.

How dare this weak-kneed crybaby tease her about her age?

"I am surprised you are leaving, Dan. In my day widowers stayed in familiar places." She said.

"Well...I...That is." He stammered to Sarah's delight. "I just need to get away for a while. Maybe someday when I come back." He pulled his watch fob out of his pocket. "It's getting late. I'm sure you are all as tired as I. Thank you again for being my friends." In the foyer, he pulled his heavy woolen coat on and said, "Wherever I go, I shall always remember you."

"And please remember that we shall always keep a room available for you." Lottie assured him.

Forty Four

Charles lit the fire as Mrs. Bramwell came through the door.

"I must speak with you." She said shyly.

"Please have a seat, Mrs. Bramwell?" He said, offering her the chief's coveted rocker. "I'll have coffee heated in just a moment."

"No thank you." She sat in the rocker and smiled at him. "I told John that I needed to be at the dressmakers this morning." She explained. "My coach is waiting at the emporium... Mr. Bowling, you said that you could be discreet?"

"Absolutely," he assured her.

"I've a confession to make." She slowly peeled off her leather gloves and held her dainty hands to the stove. "Oh don't look at me so!" She scowled. "I haven't come to tell you that I murdered my sister. But I think I was in town the day before she died. I hired a detective to find out where she was living. I wanted to tell her to leave us alone once and for all."

"And did you speak with her?" He asked, pouring himself a cup of day old coffee.

"I did. It was very early in the morning. Not even sun up. The detective, and one of John's assistants and I went there to the brothel and she came out on the front porch to see me."

"Was anyone else with her?"

"No. She told me it was her bedtime. I don't know why, but I felt nothing but pity for her, Mr. Bowling. She seemed so old and tired. I hugged her tightly and she started crying.

And for some inexplicable reason Mary pulled my locket from its chain and started yelling and screaming at me. She threatened to go the Carson City Appeal and any other newspaper that would listen to her. About that time a Chinese man came running from the back of the house telling me to leave or go to jail.

My husband's assistant was concerned lest I be recognized and ruin John's political aspirations. He jumped out of the buggy and pulled me away before she could rip my veil off. Mary refused to give me back my locket. I pleaded with her, but she was always a stubborn person. The more I begged her, the more she seemed to enjoy my predicament. In the end I had no choice but to let her keep it. Poor thing, it's all she had left in the world I suppose.

As we were walking down the steps, a woman came out the front door and told Mary that she was quickly wearing out her welcome. The Chinese man shoved Mary toward the front door and I heard him say, 'You best be careful Mary, you're liable to get in trouble.'"

She fumbled with her gloves and carefully slid them over her fingers. "I trust you will be discreet with this information?"

"You have my word." There was no reason to tell her that he'd already been told about her visit to the Silver Window.

"You told me that Joseph Hanlon had tried to extort money from you?"

She looked down at her purse. "He came to the house under the guise of looking for work."

"How did Mary find out about it?"

She smiled. "The man is so stupid. I told him I would only do business with him if he sent my sister to pick up the money. I was fairly certain that she didn't know what he was up to, but I needed to be sure. About a week later he came back to the house promising he'd never bother us again."

"I can promise you that he won't." Charles assured her.

She smiled at him.

Chief Dolan entered the office as she was leaving. He watched her cross the street and walk toward the emporium. "Mary Hanlon's sister?" He asked.

"Yes that's Mrs. Bramwell."

Dolan poured coffee in his saucer. "She's the spitting image of her." He slurped his coffee noisily. "What did she want?"

Charles told him. When he was finished Chief Dolan chuckled. "I don't doubt that she met with her sister Charlie. But I think she's lying up a storm about some of the details."

"She might be." Charles agreed.

"Especially if that meeting had took place in the canyon and she'd murdered her sister afterwards. Yessir that might be a good reason for lying."

"She did know about Wing Li and Rose."

"Just proves that she had been watching the Silver Window is all. Don't let yourself get fooled by a pretty face Charlie." Dolan said propping his boots on the desk. "It'll do you in every time."

"She looks too fragile to best anyone in a fight." Charles said.

Dolan laughed heartily. "It's them fragile ones that'll wrestle like a bear."

"All the same Chief, Mrs. Bramwell is not responsible for her sister's death."

"Hard to believe that a pretty one like her could do something so wicked, aint it?" Dolan teased.

"There's no logical reason for her to have done so." Charles said.

Dolan saw no point in arguing with his young assistant. "So what else we got facing us this morning?" He asked.

A MOTHER LODE OF MURDER

Forty Five

Therese paced back and forth. Should she hurry home and tell everyone who she had seen, or keep it to herself? The others would certainly be as shocked as she was, but did it really prove anything?

The sun had long ago risen over Sugar Loaf. With daylight, the customers were gone and the house was quiet. Everyone must be fast asleep. She didn't fear Rose and Wing Li, but neither did she want them to see her leave. She wanted to get out of this place as quickly and quietly as possible.

She stopped pacing. How would she explain what she had seen? She didn't care. It had to be done, but when. She'd worry about that later. In the meantime Therese stared at her reflection in the mirror and rubbed her face clean with a damp cloth.

Her departure would not go unnoticed. Without bothering to knock, Louise walked into her room just as she was set to make her escape.

"Where you going without your powder and rouge?" She asked flopping onto the bed.

"That is not any of your business. But if you must know, I no longer want to be here." Therese said.

"You're scared aren't you Annie?" Louise smiled. "Well you got a right to be. There's a couple murderers here in the house. "

Therese sat down on the bed beside Louise. Maybe she could coax this woman into sharing what she knew. "Who are they?"

Louise giggled. "What do you care, you're getting

out."

"Not because of any murderers."

" Well, I'm scared I'll be the next to die."

"If you truly believed that you would leave." Therese suggested. "No one in their right mind would stay around expecting to be murdered."

"Why you talking different?" Louise demanded..

"I'm not!" Therese said.

"Yes you are." Louise giggled. "You're talking like a refined woman."

"My manner of speaking is not important. Saving your life is." Therese explained. "You can get out of here if you truly want to, Louise."

"Like you?" Louise smirked.

"Yes like me. I just can't do this kind of work." Therese sighed. "It was foolish of me to think that I could."

"Where would I go?" Louise asked. "I'm not very smart. Not like Bridget and Nora and the others. I got no family or nothing. This is all I can do."

Therese wanted to shake the woman and asked what would happen to her when she got old. Instead she said. "If you don't get out you may wish you had one of these days."

"If they don't kill me," Louise laughed. "Yeah I might."

"Who are you afraid of?" Therese asked. Before Louise could answer the door opened and Bridget came in.

"Whilst you two are up here chatting, Nora and I are trying to sleep."

"Sorry." Louise murmured. "I'll get on back to

my room."

"You going somewhere, Annie?" Bridget asked.

"I hate it here and I'm leaving." Therese said. "This isn't for me."

Bridget laughed. "Rose and Wing Li might have something to say about that."

Therese stared her boldly in the eye. "They might bully all of you, but they wouldn't dare try to keep me here against my will. Because that after all, is a criminal offense." What she didn't say was that Charles would come looking for her if Sarah raised the alarm.

She pushed past Bridget and walked to the door. "I hope you will remember what I said Louise. You are free to leave the Silver Window anytime you want to do so."

"She's not going anywhere, are you Louise?"

Louise bent her head. "No."

"Even though you fear for your life?" Therese asked.

"Oh Louise," Bridget said. "You haven't been telling Annie that crazy ghosts and murder stuff again have you?"

Louise smiled. "Yes, but we was only talking."

"Did you confess to killing Mary Hanlon?" Bridget laughed.

"No, I said it was you what killed her." Louise giggled. Therese could still hear them snickering when she walked down the stairs. She was certain that one of them was afraid of someone here in the house.

Forty Six

Charles stopped onto the porch and gazed toward Six-Mile Canyon. Low slung rain clouds hovered in the distance that was the Forty-Mile Desert. Overhead the sky was white, the threat of snow looming.

He rang the bell and waited. It was too cold for the housekeeper to be outdoors scrubbing dust and dirt from the rugs. Would she open the door cradling the fat yellow cat, he wondered as he rang the doorbell again. Finally Dan opened the door smiling broadly. "Charles how long have you been out here?

He swung the door wide. "Come on in and warm yourself with a cup of coffee."

"I half expected your housekeeper--"

Dan frowned. "Hannah works when she chooses. Apparently this is one of those days she has chosen not to do so. Good help is so hard to come by these days."

Charles nodded though he'd never noticed that Lottie and Agnes had any difficulty in retaining their help. "Did you ever find the sales receipt for Miriam's earrings?" Charles asked as he followed Dan down the hallway to his study.

"I've looked high and low and haven't come across it yet." Dan said dropping into his chair.

The room was no cleaner than it was the last time he was here. He wasn't surprised the receipt hadn't turned up. "It doesn't matter."

"Can I get you coffee, anything to drink?" Dan

asked, ready to spring to his feet.

"Nothing, thank you." Charles said surveying the room's endless clutter. "Do you remember telling Chief Dolan that you had received a letter informing you of Miriam's death?"

Dan smiled. "Just vaguely. By the time our paths crossed that night I was so liquored up I could hardly stand."

"And as I recall you challenged a man to a duel."

Dan laughed. "It's a good thing he took pity on me. Otherwise I'd be up at the Virginia City Cemetery beside Theodore about now."

Dropping all pretense, Charles asked the question he'd come here to ask. "May I see that letter Dan?"

Dan sprang to his feet. "Why do you want to see that? Is it important?"

"It's crucial." Charles said. "Do you still have it?"

"Well I--I was so distraught that night there's no telling what I might have done with it."

Dan opened a desk drawer and foraged through its contents. "I thought I put it in here….No wait a minute. I recall folding it." His face was suddenly ashen." Oh my God!" He gasped. "I may have burned it."

"Why would you do such a thing?" Charles asked incredulous. "You may have needed it at some point."

"I was upset naturally. I guess by burning it I was somehow refusing to accept its message. I don't know." He absently ran his long slender fingers through his hair. "Yes! I remember now. I put it in the book I was reading that night, *The Marble Faun*, romantic gobbledygook, but it was Miriam's favorite. Most likely because one of the main characters shared her name, Miriam and Donatello, I couldn't finish reading it, "He smiled.

"Yes, I know the book, Nathanial Hawthorne." Charles said absently. "My aunt thoroughly enjoyed it. I didn't. Do you remember where you put the book?" Charles asked.

Dan turned to the book shelf and pulled the book down. Blowing on it to remove dust, he opened it. "Just as I thought, here it is."

He passed the letter to Charles, who read.

Dear Mr. Waters

It is my sad duty to inform you that your wife Miriam Margaret Waters was a registered passenger aboard the Dame Des Berges when it sank on Lake Geneva, Sunday last. Rest assured that every effort was made to rescue those on board. Sadly, there were no survivors and no bodies have been recovered at this time.

Please accept my deepest condolences. Sincerely Karl Falkenhagen Leiter der Polizei

Charles refolded the letter and asked. "May I see the envelope?"

"If I can find it, certainly." Dan said angrily. "But why you want it is beyond me."

"Do you have it?"

"Of course I do. But why is it so important?

"Please just show me the envelope Dan."

Dan opened a file and rummaged through

several envelopes. "Aha! Here it is." He said pulling the envelope from the crowded folder.

Charles carefully examined the envelope with the words Confoederatio Helvetica boldly printed on the return address. He looked at the date stamp and return address and passed the envelope back to Dan. "I'm sorry Dan. But this makes what I've got to tell you all the more strange."

"What's that?" Dan asked suddenly suspicious.

"Miriam's body was discovered in a mineshaft recently."

Dan fell onto his chair. "Have you lost your mind? Miriam died in a boat accident. You read the letter, yourself."

"This is certainly baffling and I don't understand it myself Dan." Charles said. "But I promise you this. I will find whoever killed her."

"Killed? You mean she was murdered? "

"She was stabbed to death."

No, Charles. I don't believe a word of this. You're playing some sort of sick joke." Dan snarled.

"And why would I do such a thing?" Charles asked. "I'm as shocked as you are."

Dan sunk back into his chair. "I must be certain it is Miriam. I must go see her at once."

Forty Seven

Therese slipped back into Ducks and Deeks just before breakfast.

"You two are certainly cheerful this morning." Lottie said lifting a large pancake from the platter.

"There's nothing wrong with being in a pleasant mood." Sarah snapped, reaching for a piece of bacon.

"Not at all, but we're curious why you've been laughing like a couple of schoolgirls since we came down to breakfast." Agnes said.

"It's nothing." Therese assured them. "Nothing at all."

"I've never heard either of you laugh so." Lottie said. Then turning to Charles, she asked, "Whatever is the matter dear?"

"I have something to tell you." He said, his eyes fixed on Agnes. "Very unsettling, nonetheless there's no denying it."

"What's that?" Agnes asked.

He quickly pushed a forkful of egg and potatoes into his mouth. There was no other choice. They must be told. Where to begin? Finally, he took Agnes' hand. "Mort Coombs found Miriam's body in a mineshaft near Six Mile Canyon yesterday."

"What on earth?" Agnes asked.

"I didn't believe it myself, but there it is." Charles said.

"But how can that be?" She demanded.

She leapt from her chair. "That's impossible!"

"Have you told Dan?" Lottie asked.

"He's as baffled as we are." Charles answered

"I wonder if he *is* all that surprised." Therese said.

"What are you saying?" Agnes demanded.

"Before you let your imaginations run wild, I need to tell you something." Charles said. "Yesterday I saw the letter Dan received concerning Miriam's death." He smiled at his aunt. "And yes Aunt Lottie he also showed me the envelope with its postmark and date."

"Be that as it may," Therese said, "I don't trust Dan."

"Are you daft?" Agnes asked.

"You may as well tell them now dear" Sarah coaxed.

"Tell us what?" Charles asked.

Locking eyes with Charles, Therese fell back in her chair. "For the past two days I've been at the Silver Window."

"What in blue blazes were you doing up there!" Charles demanded. "I will not put up with this—"

"Oh my goodness!" Agnes gasped.

"Charles!" Lottie admonished, "Please hear her out."

She reached to Therese and gently patted her shoulder, "It's okay dear."

Therese took a bite of muffin and said. "What does on up there is appalling. It is more outrageous than you can imagine. I saw some members of our church, half dressed and laughing it up with the women."

"Who was it?" Lottie asked, her eyes glimmering

with curiosity.

Charles stared at her angrily. "I can't believe that you would do such a goddamn stupid thing, Therese."

"Charles Bowling! You will not use the lord's name in vain!" Lottie said sternly.

"I'm sorry Aunt Lottie. I can't believe that Therese would do such a foolish thing."

"In case you haven't noticed, Charles, I'm an adult woman and able to take care of my own concerns. I went there. And what's more I--" She stopped herself. Now wasn't the time to discuss her doubts. "Those women are all horrid and mean. "Two of them seem to know who killed Mary Hanlon."

"Which women?" Charles demanded.

"Bridget and Louise." She said reaching for the butter.

"I'm certain they're frightened of someone. But it isn't Maude. I think Wing Li and Rose might be holding her prisoner. I heard her crying in her bedroom begging them to be kind to her."

"They're all such despicable characters. So why do that?" Sarah asked.

"I'm not sure." Charles said. "But I know that I've not been able to speak with her whenever I've gone there to see her."

Looking straight at Agnes, Therese said, "Speaking of despicable characters, while I was there I saw Dan carrying on with that Bridget. I can promise you that I hope to never share another meal with him."

"But why on earth would Dan--" Agnes stopped

in midsentence. "He loved Miriam."

"He has a very strange way of mourning." Therese said firmly.

"You all know that Dan Waters is not one of my favorite people," Sarah said, "but I say he deserves the benefit of the doubt. The man has endured a lot of heartache and loss recently. Enough to make a person act crazy, I suppose."

"You've given me some very helpful information, Therese. But you shouldn't have been anywhere near that place." Charles said. "If you had seen your reputation would have been ruined. And your days as a schoolteacher would be over forever."

She stood. "You're right of course. But I wanted to find some information for myself—and for your investigation of as well. I'd better be on my way to school."

She was at the door. "Wait up, Therese." Charles called. "I'll walk with you."

As they walked he reiterated what he'd told her at breakfast. "It was too big of a gamble, Therese. No investigation is worth such risks."

"I am always careful, Charles. But I can't promise that I won't take such a risk again if it means helping you out."

"We'll talk about that later. For now, I want you to tell me everything you remember about Dan and Bridget that night."

"I've already done so."

"Think!"

"She was sitting in his lap and they were laughing."

Therese closed her eyes tightly. "They were acting silly. I was trying to hide. She said something like 'my good friend Bryce.' "

"Are you sure she said Bryce and not Dan?"

"She said Bryce. But it was Dan."

"Bryce rhymes with twice." Charles said absently.

"So does mice." Theresa countered, turning and running toward the school.

Forty Eight

Benjamin's respect for Charles soared. He might be young, but he was sharp as a tack. And he meant to tell him so when he saw him again.

As the coach moved slowly up Geiger Grade, he willed the horses to gallop faster. The closer he got to Virginia City the more impatient he grew. He'd missed Mrs. Noonan's superb cooking. And he'd missed his friends at the rooming house, even Sarah with her sharp wit and sharper tongue.

Virginia City with all its dust, its noise, its riffraff and its gunplay was home. They could keep the rest of the country. As far as he was concerned there was no other place that compared to the Comstock. He would never again travel so far away, unless it involved an investigation.

He listened to the sound of the horses' hooves and of the coach's wheels rolling across the dry terrain, a monotonous tune that lulled him to sleep.

Dinner was a solemn occasion as Miriam's friends once again faced the shock of her death. Miriam hadn't been the unfortunate passenger on a doomed sightseeing boat. Instead she'd shared the same fate as the harlot Mary Hanlon.

The two women had inhabited very different worlds. This made the likelihood of a connection between their killings all the more improbable to Agnes. Still, she agreed with Charles that the same person must have murdered both women.

"There's no reason for Miriam's murder." Therese said. "Why would she suddenly turn up dead here after Dan was informed of her death halfway around the world?"

"It makes absolutely no sense." Lottie agreed. "Was she killed in the same manner as Mary Hanlon?"

All eyes were on Charles who silently shook his head.

"How then?" Sarah asked.

Charles looked to Agnes. "It's all right Charles. I've already faced the worst of it."

"She was stabbed." He said calmly.

Benjamin's arrival home was the evening's one

bright spot. Even Sarah favored him with a welcoming smile as he came through the door. After they'd share the news about Miriam, Benjamin regaled them with his stories of Monterey. And carefully withholding the reason he'd visited Mr. Pembrooke in the first place, he delighted them with the story of the elderly man's propensity for wine. In spite of their sorrow, the ladies laughed joyously as Benjamin described his subsequent headache after trying to match Pembrooke glass for glass.

Finally the ladies went to bed, leaving Charles and Benjamin free to enjoy their brandy and cigars, and to discuss certain aspects of the case neither deemed appropriate for mixed company. Benjamin puffed on his cigar and contemplated the younger man.

"By God Charles, I've got to hand it to you. You were absolutely right."

"First thing tomorrow, send an urgent telegram to Mr. Pembrooke. There is one question we need answered." Charles said.

Benjamin listened intently as Charles told him what the information he needed from the jeweler. When he was finished, Benjamin said. "This will change things somewhat. I suppose." He flicked the cigar's thick ashes in the ashtray. "Judging by their behavior, I'd say that you haven't shared your thoughts with the ladies."

"No."

Benjamin his cigar firmly in the corner of his mouth said, "That Therese is certainly one resourceful young lady." He chuckled with admiration.

"She is that." Charles agreed. "But I think we agree that for the time being it would be best if this information stays between us.

Benjamin nodded silently.

Forty Nine

Rose opened the door slowly. "You were told to leave us alone." She said.

"I'd like a word with Miss Banning." Charles said inching closer.

She grabbed the doorknob ready to close the door on him. "She is indisposed."

Ignoring her, he pushed his way into the foyer. "Please tell her I'm here…and I will not leave until I speak with her."

She scurried away silently. He walked into the parlor where a pretty young woman idly played the piano. "May I help you?" She asked.

"You are?" He asked plopping down on the velvet sofa near her.

"Nora" She smiled.

"Well Nora--"

"Nora!" Maude said as she walked into the parlor. "Please leave us alone."

The girl smiled at him and did as she was told. Charles was shocked. This couldn't be the same woman he'd spoken to only days before. Her disheveled hair was barely pinned up; the smiling lips were as pasty as her un-powdered skin. Her dress hung loosely on her. All pretense of civility was gone. Maude's brows were drawn together angrily.

"Mr. Bowling! Hasn't Farin told you to stay away from the Silver Window?"

"If you mean Chief Dolan--"

"Well I certainly didn't mean Abe Lincoln." She snarled, still pacing.

"I understand you've been ill Miss Banning and I am sorry for that. But I've got a job to do …And I mean to do it…Now will you please listen to what I have to say."

She shrugged her shoulders in capitulation. And sitting on the opposite side of the sofa from him, she said, "Very well. Tell me what it is you've come to tell me Mr. Bowling and then leave us be."

He spoke barely above a whisper. When he had finished explaining everything he had discovered she drew a deep breath. "That seems highly unlikely but you may be correct Mr. Bowling." She smiled slyly. "I haven't been paying as much attention to matters as I should lately. As a result of illness, I'm sorry to say that I allowed myself to become dependent on opium." Her hands fluttered to her face. "I must look a fright to you?"

He gallantly disagreed. She smiled and continued.

"Rose and Wing Li have been helping to wean me from the terrible ordeal of addiction." Her lower lip trembled as if she were ready to cry.

"I truly cared about Mary, for all the good that did her."

"May I count on your help?" He asked suddenly sorry for her.

"Yes." She sighed. "I feel a certain amount of responsibility for Mary's fate. If I had been more diligent and less in the throes of my addiction--"

Charles touched her hand gently. "You are in no way responsible."

Fifty

Snow fell throughout the day. By late afternoon several inches lay on the ground and a hush fell across Virginia City. Dan arrived at Ducks and Deeks smiling brightly.

Over dinner, he announced that Miriam was to be buried under the angel monument after all.

"In some ways I feel better about having her here at least." He said calmly.

"Even though you are moving on?" Sarah asked.

"Well yes. She will have all of you to honor her. I've sold the house and I--I- that is, there are too many memories here for me. I cannot stay." He daintily sliced his pork chops and added, "I'll be leaving on tomorrow's stage. It's on to Canada for me. I've always wanted to visit the wilds of Canada."

Agnes eyes filled with tears. "It's such a shame that you and Miriam couldn't have gone there together."

"Yes." He agreed. "It is."

"And here we thought she was the only one affected with wanderlust." Sarah said, helping herself to more applesauce. "One never knows."

"I wouldn't call it wanderlust." Charles said.

"Nor I." Therese agreed.

"People are different." Lottie mused. "When Doctor Duckworth died I couldn't have moved if I'd wanted to. Being around the things he owned and loved gave me a certain comfort."

"As you say people are different." Benjamin reminded her.

When they'd finished eating Charles looked at the old wall clock and said. "It's nearly six. Mrs. Lloyd ought to be here any moment to conduct a séance for us."

Lottie, Therese and Agnes were delighted. Benjamin, Sarah and Dan looked at Charles as if he'd lost his mind.

"I'll participate if it makes you happy Charles. But it's nothing but nonsense." Benjamin said and for once Sarah agreed with him.

So did Dan who said. "These women are nothing but charlatans."

"Please stay and take part with us." Lottie said to Dan. "You may change your mind."

Charles jumped at the knock on the door. Instead of Mrs. Lloyd it was the boy from the telegraph office with an urgent telegram for Benjamin.

"I hope it isn't bad news." Dan said as Benjamin headed to his room with the telegram.

"Oh dear." Agnes said wringing her hands. "Surely not."

Before they had time to further contemplate the telegram's message, there was another knock at the door. Charles opened it to Mrs. Lloyd. Whatever she spent her money on, it certainly wasn't clothing. The spiritualist arrived in the same black taffeta dress she'd worn on her previous visit. Her cape was a deep shade of purple velvet, richly embellished with floral embroidery. The ensemble was finished with matching hat and gloves. She untied her cape and hurriedly placed the candles on the table. When she was satisfied with their arrangement, she instructed them to hold hands.

"Before we begin, let me say that I will conduct our séance strictly by my mediumship. We will not use the dial tonight."

Benjamin rushed into the parlor. "Sorry for the interruption, may I join you?"

She nodded coldly, and then looking at each of the others, she said. "If everyone is ready we shall commence."

Satisfied by their silent stares, she bowed her head. "Tonight we call only positive spirits who come to us in love and in light." She drummed her hands on the table. "Let us attempt to call in the spirits by tipping the table. Table up!" She commanded rubbing her large hands across the mahogany parlor table's rich patina. "Table up! Table up! Table up!"

"Apparently the spirits aren't interested in table tipping tonight." She explained lighting the candles. "Spirits we beseech you speak to us!" She commanded.

The candles flickered wildly. "Ah. I see we have a spirit present. Might I ask your name?"

She gasped. "Mary Hanlon! Is that you?"

Sarah looked around the table nervously. Surely this woman couldn't really be speaking to the dead woman.

"Is it really Mary?" Lottie asked. "I don't see how."

"Tell us who killed you." Benjamin urged the spirit.

"Wait!" Mrs. Lloyd held up a hand. "There are two spirits present! One is Mary the other is Miriam?"

"Oh!" gasped Agnes. "Dear sweet Miriam."

"I--I—very well then," Mrs. Lloyd said. "I will tell them." She looked directly at Charles. "Mr. Bowling, Miriam wishes to give you a private message concerning her death." She dropped her head to the table a moment. "She is gone." Suddenly the spiritualist raised her head and stared at the wall. She shuddered as the color drained from her face.

"I apologize Mr. Eldons. I didn't see you there." She nodded her head several times. "Of course it was your daughter." She shook her head. "No! I cannot do that. Please don't ask it of me."

"What does he want Mrs. Lloyd?" Charles asked.

"Mr. Eldons wants me to call Miriam to him. He says that he shall name his killer in due time and wishes me to tell you that he will not rest in peace until this person is brought to justice."

"His killer?" Benjamin demanded. "How is Charles supposed to do that if he doesn't know who it is?"

Mrs. Lloyd sobbed. "Oh my goodness!" She stared at Charles. "Mr. Eldons says that you already know the killer's identity and that you must act upon your knowledge quickly lest he escape. No..No that doesn't make sense. Very well I will say it. She was forced to kill twice for love." The spiritualist looked up. "He is gone...May we have some lights please?"

Dan and Benjamin stared at the spiritualist incredulously. "Amazing. Truly amazing." Benjamin said. "What was Eldons talking about? He died of a heart attack."

Charles jumped up and relit the lights. "When shall you give me that private message?" He asked.

"I wonder though--" Agnes said.

"She suggests we meet at the cemetery gates."

"In this weather?" Benjamin asked. "I'd say that's extremely inconsiderate of her."

"Perhaps spirits aren't bothered by the elements." Sarah suggested. And to everyone's amazement they shared a hearty laugh.

"I hardly think this is any laughing matter." Agnes admonished them, wiping her eyes.

"I am merely the medium. The messenger if you will." Mrs. Lloyd assured them. "These spirits have given you a message, Mr. Bowling. How you choose to act upon it is none of my concern."

"But when? When shall we meet?" Charles asked.

"Saturday at noon." The spiritualist said packing the candles in the satchel. Charles noticed that her hands trembled as her helped her with her cape. "Wonderful séance, Mrs. Lloyd." He assured her.

As her coach pulled away from the rooming house Dan stood and yawned. "That was a load of bosh. That woman is nothing but a very gifted liar. I was there when Theodore died. And believe me, it was a heart attack that took him."

"Of course Dan, but what if Miriam really does have a message for Charles?" Agnes asked. "I believe it could be possible."

Dan laughed. "You do? I think this woman makes her money by duping people into believing a lot of nonsense." He looked to Benjamin for confirmation.

"It won't hurt to go there and see what transpires." Benjamin said.

"I suppose not." Dan smirked. "If you don't mind wasting your time Charles."

Charles nodded. 'It can't hurt to hear what she says."

"Perhaps." Dan replied slipping into his overcoat. Then turning to Lottie he said, "Thank you again Lottie, Agnes. Until tomorrow, my friends."

Lottie closed the door behind him and said. "Dan's purchased that Inverness quite recently."

"A fashionable coat, and very popular with

gentlemen." Agnes said.

"I've always suspicioned that there was a bit of a fop in Dan." Sarah sniffed. Except for Martin Harris with his effusive compliments, any man that dressed according to the dictates of fashion was a fop in her eyes.

"Well, I doubt that I shall ever feel the same for him, knowing that he was at that bawdy house cavorting with those fallen women."

"And sadly, neither shall I." Agnes agreed.

Fifty One

Sunshine sparkled on the freshly fallen layer of snow. Charles picked at his food in silence.
"Are you ill dear?" Lottie asked, pouring herself a hot cup of cocoa.

He shook his head. "I'm thinking."

Therese buttered a biscuit and asked. "About the murder?"

He nodded.

"Which one?" Sarah asked.

"Both of them." Charles said.

Agnes looked up from the newspaper. "Mrs. Lloyd will be giving another séance at Piper's next week. Anyone care to go again?"

"Not me." Benjamin said. "I've had enough of that woman and her séances."

"I'll wait until Jenny Lind returns." Sarah said.

"Such a lovely voice." Benjamin agreed.

"Why so gloomy, Charles?" Therese asked.

"It's nothing." He lied.

Sarah reached for a muffin. "As I recall, you always get like this when you are ready to make an arrest. So who is it? Who is going to the gallows…do you know?"

"I believe I do." Charles said.

Chief Dolan had endured enough crime for one day. He was old and tired, and wanted only to go home. But what Charles had to tell him couldn't wait. He poured himself another cup of coffee and hunched over the stove. With any luck, he'd be home before snow started falling again. He slid his spectacles on and reread the telegram again. "Looks like you were right boy."

"I certainly didn't want to be." Charles said. And as he laid out the circumstances of the crimes, Dolan listened intently. Finally he said. "Yessir, this is a goddamn shock if ever there was one."

Charles nodded. "I believe Mary Hanlon inadvertently witnessed something she shouldn't have. And they felt they had no choice but to kill her."

"I reckon so." Dolan said. "Will you be needing me to make the arrest?"

"Not unless you want to." Charles said.

"Promise me you won't let them escape Charlie."

"I don't intend to."

The chief contemplated him. "I expect you to put a bullet in their brains if it is your only choice. Can you do that?"

Without hesitation Charles answered. "Yes."

"Then I reckon I'll go on home." Dolan said stretching. "Looks like Martin Harris might get his big trial after all."

Fifty Two

Benjamin had finished *War and Peace* and was now engrossed with Wilkie Collins' *The Moonstone*. Moving his chair closer to the fireplace, he concentrated on solving the case of heroine Rachel Verinder's stolen diamond. He turned the pages as quickly as he read, he was Sergeant Cuff and he'd walked the mean streets of London.

Therese absently played the piano lost in her own thoughts. Charles studied his notes.

Agnes and Lottie played cards and Sarah busily knitted. Dan did not come this evening. It was too cold and besides, he abhorred tearful good-byes, he'd explained. When the card game was over Charles looked pointedly at Agnes and said. "Before I tell you that I've solved the murders—"

"With our help." Therese reminded him.

Yes, with your help." He said looking at Benjamin.

"Just tell them." Benjamin said closing his book. He'd get back to it when he could. But for now the Moonstone would have to remain unsolved.

Charles closed his notebook. "About Miriam's death--"

"What about it?" Agnes asked.

" I'll be making an arrest tomorrow."

"Who?" Agnes asked.

Charles said. "Before I do that, let me explain what--

"Damn it! Who did it?" Sarah demanded.

"There were two people involved. That's the

only thing that makes sense." He sighed.

"Rose and Wing Li?" Lottie asked.

"It was Dan and Bridget, the woman up at the bawdy house.

Lottie gasped. "No!"

"Yes Aunt Lottie."

Agnes jumped up. "Oh no Charles! You're mistaken. That's impossible. Dan wouldn't do such a terrible thing. Benjamin you know Dan couldn't kill anyone."

"That's not what the evidence is saying, Agnes." Benjamin said calmly.

"Let's not forget that I saw him at the bawdy house," Therese said. "And he certainly didn't seem like the bereaved widow to me. To think he sat here in this very parlor with us and cried for her."

"Going to a bawdy house doesn't make one a killer." Lottie said. "Otherwise half the men in this town are killers."

"Are you sure it wasn't an accident? Maybe she came home and fell--"

Charles shook his head. "And stabbed herself? No Agnes it wasn't like that. Miriam was murdered." He said gently trying to remind her of what he'd already told her.

"There's no question about Dan?" Lottie asked.

"None whatsoever," He answered. "Agnes, you said that Dan gave Miriam the ruby earrings as a gift when he returned from a business trip?'

"That's what she told me."

"But the jeweler told Benjamin that both Mr. and Mrs. Waters purchased those earrings. Now why would Miriam lie about that, I wondered."

"She wouldn't!" Agnes said. "Miriam was not a liar."

"And I realized that. My dilemma was Miriam's honesty. She prided herself on her truthfulness. And she would never have lied about a pair of earrings, but someone was lying. The jeweler who designed them had no reason to lie about who his customer was."

At a nod from Charles, Benjamin took over the explanation. "I sent a telegram asking Mr. Pembrooke to describe Mrs. Waters, here is his reply. 'Mrs. Waters lovely...aged early 20s, tall, slender. Beautiful green eyes thick black hair.' "

He turned to Therese. "Who fits this description?"

She gasped. "Bridget!"

"That is also an apt description of the Eldon caretaker/housekeeper Hannah." Lottie said.

"Bridget and Hannah are one in the same." Charles said." He turned to Therese. "After you told me what happened at the brothel, I watched Bridget and Dan. I saw her going back and forth from his house a few times."

"Of course!" Agnes said. "I remember now. I caught a glimpse of her as she was leaving the church. You told me who she was and that she'd left some of Miriam's dresses. Do you recall that Lottie? Then at Piper's I saw her again sitting in the fallen dove box. I knew that I had seen her somewhere, but I couldn't place her."

"But why buy two identical pairs of earrings?" Sarah asked.

"I'm not sure." Charles said. "But I do know that both Miriam and Bridget wore them."

"I knew it!" Sarah exclaimed. "He gave himself away the night he came to dinner while Therese was at the--" She smiled. "I meant to tell you Charles, but it slipped my mind until now. Agnes do you recall Dan saying that she is so clever, she often designs her own clothing and her own jewelry?"

"Yes, but what does it prove?" Agnes asked.

"He used the present tense. And if you recall that was the only time he'd done so since her death. He realized his mistake and commenced weeping so as to change the subject."

"Besides which, Miriam couldn't even draw a straight line. And Dan didn't say 'Miriam was so gifted' He said, 'she is so gifted' "

"He was talking about that Bridget." Sarah said.

"A thoroughly evil woman, that's who Louise was trying to warn me about," Therese said. "It was obvious that she was afraid of someone and every time she tried to tell me there was Bridget consoling her."

"Not consoling her so much as threatening her." Charles said. "The same thing happened the day I showed them the earring. Louise recognized it right away, but was afraid to tell me. She broke down sobbing to Bridget that she didn't want to die."

. "You told me that you heard Bridget calling Dan Bryce. And that made me think. Do you recall what the Coombs said about hearing two people in a buggy? He said that one of those people was saying that the other made a murderer of him twice. What if one of them was actually saying, 'you've made a murderer of me Bryce.'?" Many people go by their middle names. And apparently Dan goes by his middle name Bryce in certain circles. I think the Coombs heard Bridget complaining about the killings. "

"Do you suppose--" Lottie stopped herself. "Not Theodore. Surely they didn't kill him as well."

"Yes Aunt Lottie, they did. Didn't you notice Dan's expression when Mrs. Lloyd began her conversation with Eldons? "

"A nice bit of acting." Benjamin said. "But proving that they killed him will be impossible unless one of them confesses."

"I think the Coombs heard an argument between Dan and Bridget that night after they'd killed Mary. Mr. Coombs heard someone say 'You have made a murderer of me, twice'. This really didn't make much sense to me until I remembered that Bryce is Daniel's middle name. And you Therese heard her calling him Bryce. She was saying you have made a murderer of me, Bryce, not twice.

"But Mrs. Coombs said they were speaking Chinese?" Lottie said.

"And Mr. Coombs said her hearing isn't what it once was." Charles reminded her.

"I told you she couldn't tell the difference between Chinese and a barn owl." Sarah sniffed.

"But why did they kill Mary Hanlon?" Therese asked.

"Because she stumbled onto them, that's the only thing that makes sense to me.

I asked Mrs. Lloyd to return last night so that we could set a trap for Dan. Hopefully I'll catch them before they get away."

"Aren't you afraid they might try to kill Mrs. Lloyd before she has the opportunity to give you Miriam's spirit message?" Sarah asked.

Charles laughed. "Yes I was concerned for her safety. That's why I had one of the night shift men take her to his home. She is spending time with his mother while he is acting as bait at the Lloyd house."

He patted Therese's hand. "If not for Benjamin going to Monterey and you going up to the bawdy house they might have gotten away with it."

. "I knew we could help you with this case. Hopefully Martin Harris won't put me on the witness stand and force me to tell the whole city about my time at the brothel."

"First he'd have to know what you know." Benjamin said. "And since no one here is going to tell him--"

"Of course we aren't going to tell anyone about your er uh, time at the brothel" Lottie assured her. "That shall forever remain a secret among your dearest friends."

Beaming Therese said, "I don't know what I'd do without the five of you."

"Do you think Dan will swing?" Benjamin asked.

"I hope so." Sarah said. "If anyone deserves to go to the gallows it's Dan Waters."

"And what about her? Bridget deserves to swing also." Therese said.

"True enough." Benjamin agreed. "But doubtful.

No, Bridget will spend the rest of her days in prison. It's a pity. In my estimation she is as guilty as he is."

"Yes she certainly is." Charles agreed. "Miriam was mistakenly listed on the passenger manifest. Or she may have registered and then changed her mind. When she realized what had happened she came home to surprise Dan. Instead, he killed her."

Agnes sobbed. "How could he do such a thing to Miriam?"

"I don't think he planned it that way. They were just in it for the money. They were probably going to take all the money and disappear before Miriam returned. Her death in the boat accident must have seemed like the perfect opportunity. Now there was no rush. They could rob Miriam's estate at leisure. Imagine how they felt when she suddenly reappeared alive and healthy."

"Miriam loved him so." Agnes howled.

"Now dear, you mustn't upset yourself." Lottie said, gently touching her friend's shoulder. "Charles will make sure that he pays for what he's done."

Fifty Three

While the others slept, they sneaked out to the B. Street Livery. Sarah and Benjamin, the most unlikely of allies, had joined forces. The air was frigid. Puffs of vapor escaped from their mouths each time they spoke. Any other day the biting cold might have wreaked havoc with rheumatism and old bones, but not today. This morning they had a plan. And that was to catch a ruthless killer.

Benjamin woke the stable hand while Sarah stood guard lest someone from the house come looking for them. That was unlikely. Except for the miners laboring far beneath the earth, the rowdy bunch of men just off duty, and the all night drinkers and gamblers, Virginia City slept.

Benjamin gallantly helped Sarah into the buggy and spryly, for a man his age, jumped in.

"We will need to find someplace to hide." He said as the buggy neared the cemetery.

She pointed to a thick patch of juniper bushes. "Maybe over there."

"Too far away." He said. "My eyes aren't what they once were."

"Nor mine." She agreed. "So I brought my opera glasses."

He snapped the reigns and urged the horses slowly down the hill. "Good thing you thought of that."

Benjamin pulled the buggy up behind a stand of junipers.

"Now we wait." He said, pulling his hat down over his eyes.

Sarah couldn't sleep; excitement surged through her. Time moved slowly. Minutes dragged on. The sun was halfway up Sugar Loaf and Benjamin was snoring softly. She nudged him sharply in the ribs. "Look!" she whispered. "There's someone moving over there. It looks like he has a rifle."

Benjamin pulled his hat up and squinted in the direction she pointed. Staring through the opera glasses he said, "He's set to shoot Charles and Mrs. Lloyd ...Wait a minute. Take a look."

Sarah held the glasses to her eyes. "That's a woman!"

While they stared at the rifleman someone crept up behind them. Benjamin pulled his pistol.

"I might have known I'd find you two out here." Charles scowled, climbing into the buggy with them. "We'll discuss the danger you've put yourselves in later. See anything?"

Benjamin holstered his gun. "A woman with a rifle, probably waiting for you and the spiritualist, here take a look."

Charles took the glasses and held them to his eyes. "Just as I thought."

"Who is it?" Sarah demanded.

"I believe she's Dan's accomplice."

"Accomplice? You mean Bridget?" Benjamin asked.

"If I'm right...." He said.

"See the buggy at the cemetery entrance?"

"Whoever's in it is a sitting duck!" Benjamin said.

Charles chuckled. "Two of Mrs. Darlington's dressmaker dummies, I doubt they'll complain much."

"No, but she might." Sarah said.

"I paid full price for them." Charles said.

Suddenly the rifleman raised the gun and fired wildly at the cemetery. Charles grabbed the opera glasses and stared in the distance. "Doesn't she see that buggy? What the hell is she shooting at?"

The rifleman turned the gun. They were surrounded by gunfire and bullets ricocheting off nearby rocks. Benjamin pushed Sarah to the floor of the buggy. "Stay down!" He ordered.

Just as quickly as it had erupted, the gunfire stopped. "You all right Sarah?" Charles asked.

She raised her head and looked around. "Pshaw! It'll take more than that evil vixen to frighten me."

"I'll follow her." Charles said jumping from the buggy.

"What should we do?" Benjamin asked.
"Go home and let the others know what happened. They may be wondering."

"We can help if need be. We're too old and wise to be afraid!" Benjamin said

Sarah nodded her agreement.

"I can handle it from here." Charles said.

Disappointment registered on their faces. "Are you sure you don't need us?" Benjamin asked taking the reins.

"Can't we stay and help you capture them?" Sarah asked.

"Right now I need you to go home and be safe, Sarah."

"If that's what you want." She sighed.

Benjamin snapped the rein, urging the horses to action. "See you back at the house." He called as the buggy slowly rolled away.

Charles mounted his horse and raced toward the Silver Window. She was cunning and cold-blooded. She must be stopped at all costs. It would be easy for her to make her escape and start anew somewhere else. Eventually she would kill again. Her kind always did. He pounded on the brothel's door.

As Rose opened it he shoved his way in. And racing toward the kitchen he called, "Who just came in?"

"One of the girls." She answered, sullenly.

"Which one?" He demanded.

"I--I'm not sure." She stammered. "They come in and out that back door all the time. We stopped trying to prevent--"

"I don't care about that!" He said. "I want to know who it was!"

"It was me!" Bridget said stepping from the corner.

" I had hoped I was wrong about you, Bridget."

She taunted. "Oh I'm sure you did, Mr. Bowling."

He angrily grabbed her arm, digging his fingers into the soft flesh. "Why were you shooting at my friends and me near the cemetery?"

"Stop it!" She screamed. "You're hurting me."

"Where's the gun?" He asked, still holding onto her.

"I tossed it in the sagebrush."

He loosened his grip, "So which is it, Bridget or Hannah?

She laughed wildly. "What does it matter to you?

You're the same as all the rest of them. You and your sanctimonious pretense of solving Mary's murder, you might have some people believing in you, but I never could.

Every time you came and asked Louise and me the same questions over and over...I knew. Charles Bowling special assistant to Police Chief Dolan, ha! Louise and I enjoyed some good laughs at your expense."

"That's good because you won't find much humor where you're going."

"Oh Charles," she mocked. "Why don't you just let me leave? You know you don't want to see anything happen to me."

"You helped murder three innocent people. You deserve to be behind bars."

"You've got nothing on me. No one's told you anything."

"Oh I've got plenty on you Bridget. Do you recall Louise's reaction when I showed you the earring?"

"What of it?" She smirked.

"She saw you wearing it the night Mary Hanlon was murdered and when she gets in a court of law, she'll tell it."

She sank to her knees. "That old man and woman didn't matter a whit to me. But Mary was different; I didn't want him to kill her. He wouldn't listen."

"Who?" He demanded.

Rose stared at Bridget horror stricken.

"You killed Mary?"

Bridget leapt to her feet. Shrieking wildly she ran toward the hall and up the staircase. Charles followed, taking the stairs two at a time. Her pitiful sobs filled the hallway as she dashed into her room, locking the door behind her. He pounded on the door. "Unlock this door at once!"

"Leave me be," she cried.

"There's no place left to run."

"I begged him not to do it." She sobbed. "He…he said we had no choice. She'd heard too much. Mary was my friend. I didn't want him to kill her…But I love him so."

"Open the door Bridget. We can talk about it." Charles coaxed.

"It's all over now." She cried. "We knew that we had to get away before--"

"Before we found Miriam's body?" He asked.

"You would never have found her if not for those old fools and their dog. Bryce and I, we were so happy… she was dead and we were finally free. But there was a mistake. When she came home and found us embracing in the parlor. We told her we could explain everything if she would just go with us to the canyon. She was so stupid. She believed us." Bridget giggled. "She went out there with us and I-- he couldn't do it. So I did it. Then we shoved her in the mineshaft."

He'd unraveled that much of the puzzle. "What did Mary Hanlon hear?" He demanded.

"The night wasn't that cold. So we were out at the rock. We were arguing about murdering old man Eldons with his pillow. He was very kind to me and I was feeling bad for killing him…Bryce said not to feel that way. It was something that had to be done…and now we could get the money and leave. We thought we were alone…until Mary started coughing."

He thought of Theodore Eldons struggling for air, and of Mary Hanlon, killed because of two people's greed. "Money meant that much to you?"

"You don't understand. Bryce is my world—Oh please, please tell him that I love him even now. Bryce, I love you and I always will!" She howled.

"You can tell him yourself." Charles said.
Suddenly a piercing scream and the sounds of retching came from the room. Charles listened at the door. "Bridget…Bridget are you in there?"

Wing Li came scampering up the stairs with Dan Waters right behind him. "I'm sorry, Mr. Bowling. It took me some time to locate the right key," He said putting put it in the lock.

Bridget would not be going to prison after all. She was sprawled on the floor; an empty bottle lay beside her. Vomit covered her chin and dress. Her mouth frothed. Charles had seen the symptoms of strychnine poisoning before.

Dan pushed past Charles and bent over the dead woman, sobbing.
"Hannah my love get up, get up now. It's me, Bryce." He cried.

"She's gone, Dan." Charles said.

"Is she dead?" Dan shrieked.

Charles nodded. "Strychnine. No one could have saved her."

Dan gasped for air like someone who's had the wind knocked from them. Shoving Wing Li aside, he bolted for the door, raced down the stairs and out the back door. Charles would not let him escape.

He leapt on his horse and gave chase. Their horses galloped full speed down D. Street to Union. Dan's mare was faster than Charles' bay, but Charles was gaining ground. The horses slowed as they made their way up the steep hill toward Piper's Opera House, and Charles caught up with Dan.

At Piper's Dan dismounted and raced into the empty building. He jumped up on the stage as Charles entered the building.

"Come on down off the stage. It's all over, Dan." Charles called.

Dan pulled a pistol from his pocket and held it to his head. "I'm about to rob you and all the good citizens of the pleasure of watching me hang."

"That's not the answer." Charles said. "What you and Bridget did was heinous, but killing yourself will only add to the number of deaths on your conscience." He didn't believe his words even as he spoke them. If there were a hell, Dan and Bridget would surely burn there forever, regardless of how they met their own deaths.

"We had you fooled for a long time." Dan boasted.

"For a while," Charles agreed. "Your red eyes…I thought they were red from crying over your father-in-law and then your wife. When I saw that your housekeeper was a cat lover and you commented that you didn't allow the creature in the house. I wondered…You see, I have the same allergies to cats. Do you remember that day I visited you house with the earring, Dan?"

Dan nodded.

"You knocked on the window but your housekeeper didn't turn and respond to you. Instead she ignored you. She put the cat down and went back to work on the rug...When you told me she wasn't deaf I started thinking. Why did she ignore you? She didn't want to risk me seeing her. Why was that? Because she knew that I would recognize her."

"When you showed up at the house with that earring, we knew our goose was cooked. If you hadn't stumbled upon Miriam, we would have gotten clean away."

"Maybe," Charles agreed. "One thing I don't understand. Why did you have identical earrings designed for your wife and your paramour?"

"Actually that wasn't how things were meant to be." Dan laughed, waving the gun. "Hannah loved the ruby earrings so much she ordered herself two pairs. She was always losing something and wanted to make sure her earrings were safe. I was to put the extra pair in my safe deposit box when I returned to Virginia City. Unfortunately Miriam went snooping and found the box in my things. At that point I had no choice but to say the earrings were a surprise gift for her." He shrugged his shoulders. "Woman are odd creatures at times. When I told Hannah she laughed about it, and said it might be fun to wear the same specially designed earrings at the bawdy house that Miriam was wearing to the church socials. I didn't see the humor in it. But that's a woman for you."

"Was her real name Bridget or was it Hannah?" Charles asked.

Dan cocked the pistol and began to sob. "Hannah!" He yelled. "She was…the only woman I have ever truly loved."

Charles flinched in sorrow for Miriam, trapped in a loveless marriage with a heartless man who had never cared for her. The knowledge that she meant so little to her husband is what sent Miriam on her travels.

"You married Miriam for her father's money." Charles said.

"Are you daft?" Dan chuckled. "Of course I married her for the money. Here was this wealthy woman desperately in love with me and wanting to be my wife." He smiled. "What else could I do but marry her?"

"But you were already married to Hannah." Charles sneered.

"It took you long enough to figure that out." Dan laughed. "It was a brilliant scheme don't you think? Hannah following me here and going to work at the Silver Window was her idea. I could see her nearly every night and no one was the wiser. I was just another customer as far as they were concerned."

"She was your wife and the only woman you ever loved, yet you permitted her to work in a bawdy house." Charles said with disgust.

"Hannah and I were not bound by foolish morals."

Charles glared at the man he had once considered a friend. He had arrested a lot of murderers and never had he wanted to see someone hang for their crimes more than he did at this moment.

"You pointed me toward your scheme when you told me you purchased the earrings in Monterey." He said. "Did you think I wouldn't check?"

"I was your poor pathetic suffering friend." Dan chided. "As long as I wept for the dearly departed Miriam I felt that Hannah and I were reasonably safe from your brilliant skills of detection." He chuckled. "I must say that the séance by Mrs. Lloyd was superbly choreographed. Good job Charles! She put on an excellent performance."

He paced across the stage. "There's one bit of irony here that I don't want lost to you. It was Miriam herself who hired Hannah as our housekeeper/caretaker. She liked her on sight. Said she had intelligence and spirit. I played the doubtful one and made a great show of questioning Hannah's skills. But Miriam was the sort of woman who always had to have the last word. Naturally she prevailed. It made it so easy for us to put our plan into action. In the evening I visited her at the Silver Window and she sneaked out during the day to be with me."

"Your plan? Surely you are not attempting to blame her for these three killings. This was all your doing Dan. To get what you wanted, you murdered three people in cold blood." Charles said calmly. "Hannah was your accomplice."

"Why Charles, you're not nearly as smart as you think you are." Dan smirked. "Hannah was greedy." He laughed. "She wanted the money and she didn't care who she had to kill to get it. I admit only to killing that trollop out in the canyon, but it was Hannah who killed Theodore. She smothered the old fool with his own pillow. When she realized that I just couldn't kill Miriam, she stepped up with that silver dagger of hers and finished the job. She did it because we loved one another. Now that she's gone I have nothing."

"You still have your addiction to opium." Charles reminded him coldly.

"So you know about that, do you?"

"Someone saw you down in Wo Sing's den."

"That bitch Maude Banning, no doubt. The old crone is as addicted as I am."

"It was Benjamin."

"And he never said a word…"

"He told me." Charles said calmly. "We felt pity for you. With you father in law dead and your wife halfway across the world, if opium was your one vice, so be it."

"How very kind of you," Dan said.

Put the gun away Dan and come down off the stage."

"Martin Harris would like that, wouldn't he?" Dan chuckled. "You can tell the pompous ass that I'm sorry to disappoint him." And inching closer to the stage's edge, he asked. "One thing I must know. What did Hannah say about me? Did she mention me in her last moments?"

Charles would not give succor to this ruthless killer. "She didn't say anything about you."

"Nothing?" Dan asked. "Are you certain?"

"She didn't say one word about you Dan." The lie was the only earthly retribution Dan Waters would ever receive. Charles turned away at the horrible, shrieking animal's cry. Let him take his broken heart straight to hell.

Dan put the gun against his temple. "Don't try to stop me!"

"I won't." Charles assured him. "This is what you deserve."

The explosive sound of gunfire echoed through the building. Dan's body fell to the floor with a thud, leaving Charles in the icy silence of the empty opera house.

He stepped out of the opera house and gazed down at C. Street. The sun was almost gone. Soon the city's thin façade of civility would be torn away. Saloons would fill with the raucous laughter of miners just up from the earth, safe and alive for another day. Sucking on their cigars, gamblers would hunch over Faro tables and pray for luck. Haggard women would hide in the shadows and offer an hour's worth of pleasure for the price of a decent meal. Pianos and banjos would assail the ears with lively melodies that pretended to take the edge off one's misery. Anger would turn into gunfights. And death would come, as it always did, like a hungry tabby cat stalking its prey.

The chief would be relieved the murder was solved and the case concluded. Maude Banning could breathe easily. No hint of scandal would befall her or the Silver Window. She wouldn't have to cry on the shoulders of her powerful friends after all.

Denied his first murder conviction, Martin Harris would demand a full accounting. He could console himself knowing that more murders would be committed. Therese and the others would want to hear every detail. For the next week they would talk of little else except Dan Waters and how he had fooled them all.

Charles reminded himself to stop at Mrs. Lloyd's and thank her for helping him nab the killers. He was glad he'd given her more pay than she had asked for. She deserved it. She'd done an excellent job of acting during the séance. Then again, there was always the possibility that she'd actually been speaking with old man Eldons. He dismissed the thought as nonsense. It was easier that way.

His stomach gurgled, reminding him that it was dinnertime and he was hungry. Charles climbed upon his horse. And urging the bay toward Ducks and Deeks, he remembered that it was Sunday. Mrs. Noonan would have roast beef and all the trimmings ready and waiting.

Other books by Janice Oberding

Haunted Virginia City
Haunted Reno
The Boy Nevada Killed
Haunted Lake Tahoe
The Haunting of Las Vegas
The Ghosts of Goldfield and Tonopah
Demon Song
Tiptoe Through the Tombstones
A Death in Tonopah
Abracadaver
The Woman Who Wanted Everything (erotica)
Nevada Noir
Dancing with the Dahlia
The Mizpah Hotel, History Happenings and Hauntings
(with Virginia Ridgway)
Haunted Nevada
Ouija Strange but True
Haunted Valentine

Made in the USA
Monee, IL
14 June 2024